POX

ANGELA PEARSE

© 2024 by Angela Pearse

The moral right of the author has been asserted.
All rights reserved.
No part of this book may be reproduced or used in any manner without written permission of the copyright owner.
First paperback edition May 2024.
Published by Clamp Ltd. (clamp.pub)

Set in Work Sans and Sabon.
Cover art by My Lan Khuc Valle.

ISBN 978-1-914531-82-8 Paperback (KDP)
ISBN 978-1-914531-83-5 (Ingram Spark)

Smallpox was always present, filling the churchyards with corpses, tormenting with constant fears all whom it had not yet stricken, leaving on those whose lives it spared the hideous traces of its power, turning the babe into a changeling at which the mother shuddered, and making the eyes and cheeks of the betrothed maiden objects of horror to the lover.

(Thomas Macaulay, English historian, 1694)

Chapter 1

Oxford, present day

'Anna, I'm leaving.'

Becca's words filtered into my Monday morning brain fog, but I didn't fully comprehend their meaning. I sipped my coffee, unconcerned. 'I'm not sure why I need to know you're going to the loo. But thanks for telling me.'

There was a silence, and I glanced over to the adjoining desk. Becca's face had taken on a patient expression, as a mother's might when dealing with a small child. Oh, OK, that wasn't what she meant. Despite being a senior researcher with a doctoral in history who could rattle off all sorts of facts and figures, sometimes I failed to understand basic communication.

My stomach dropped as her real meaning sunk in. 'What? But you can't leave. I need you, and I've just gotten used to you!'

Becca had been hired fresh out of her master's degree six

months ago as my research assistant for Professor Jeremy Trelawny's book *The Impact of Smallpox on Eighteenth-Century England.*

Despite a three-year age gap, we'd bonded over endless cups of tea and a shared fascination with endemic diseases. Becca's caustic wit reminded me of my twin sister, Beth. Plus she had the same first initial and our long dark hair, slim build, and green eyes. Not that I'd seen Beth for two years. She might have shaved her head, put on 100 pounds, and now wear coloured contacts for all I knew ...

Becca hitched a shoulder and looked sheepish. 'As much as I like working with you, I've had a great offer—a three-month research post in Africa.'

'Africa!' I screeched a touch too loud, and Becca winced.

'Wow,' I said in a softer tone. 'Doing what?'

'Collecting oral histories from people affected by malaria and documenting their personal experiences related to the disease,' she explained. 'It's something I've always wanted to do. And my time working on the pox project boosted my application to the top of the pile.'

I folded my arms, frowning at her. 'Does Jeremy know about this?'

'Yes, he was the one who acted as my referee. I didn't want to say anything to you until I was sure, but I got confirmation over the weekend.'

Jeremy hadn't mentioned anything to me about Becca leaving. But then again, there was a hierarchy in the faculty—one I was duly aware of at times like this. Information tended to flow upwards or sideways and only down the chain when strictly necessary. But still ... Becca was *my* assistant, and I'd miss her.

A thought struck. What if Jeremy hired someone unbearable to replace her? We shared a small office, and I wasn't great with other people in my personal space. I needed quiet and calm to do my job. A foot tapper, gum chewer, or loud headphones-music player would irritate the heck out of me. There was also the worry he'd hire a woman I couldn't compete with. Becca, once I'd gotten used to her little quirks, was safe as she was ensconced in a long-term relationship. And as far as I knew, she didn't find Jeremy remotely attractive; she'd never said anything to me anyway.

'Has he ...' I started, and Becca knew instantly where my mind was headed.

'Begun advertising? Yes, since I'm on my notice period starting today.' She moved her mouse, clicked on a link, and brought up the history faculty vacancies page in case I was still in denial. 'See?'

I leaned over and saw the listing: 'Assistant Required for Senior Researcher on Smallpox Project'. Below it was a brief paragraph about the role, qualifications required, along with salary and start date.

This was turning out to be a bad day. I should have stayed in bed and skipped Monday altogether.

'Maybe you should leave too,' said Becca casually. I almost choked on a mouthful of lukewarm coffee.

'Me? Why would I leave? I'm doing important work.'

'Yes, but you've been doing it for two years. Don't you want to branch out and do something else? There are lots of interesting positions on here. You should take a look.'

I shook my head emphatically. 'Jeremy's book requires meticulous research, and I wouldn't want to leave him in the lurch, especially as he's about to start writing. He needs me for editing, cross-referencing, and footnotes.'

What was she even thinking suggesting I leave?

Becca was looking at me with a curious, almost-knowing glint in her eye. 'Are you sure it's the book you're focused on?'

'I don't know what you mean.' I averted my gaze and concentrated on the document displayed on my computer screen. I was combing through church records in south-east England from 1749 to 1779. They were proving vital because some months had disturbingly high deaths from smallpox. It was fascinating stuff (well, to me).

'Come on, Anna. I've seen the way you go all moony

whenever you're around him,' said Becca in a strange voice.

I glanced sideways and saw that she'd puckered her lips and was fluttering her eyelashes. She looked ridiculous. I threw a paper clip at her. 'I don't do that!'

But inside, I quailed. God, if Becca had noticed, who else had? Jeremy himself? I shuddered to think of it. I thought I'd been pretty discreet at keeping my feelings to myself. Obviously, I had a bad poker face.

I took another sip of coffee, now cold and acrid, and swallowed it down, hoping she'd drop the subject.

But Becca, whose features had returned to normal, was warming up to the subject. 'I mean, I can see the appeal. He's good-looking, smart, and charming. But he's a chronic serial dater. You must've noticed that. No one is ever good enough. If they get a second date with him, they're lucky. A third date is a miracle. But he never takes it any further.'

'There's nothing wrong with being picky,' I said resolutely. 'He's just trying to find the right person—'

The landline on my desk rang, interrupting me, and my cheeks tingled with the start of a blush. I'd privately labelled my phone the 'Jeremy hotline' since he was the only one who ever rang me on it.

Becca mouthed 'serial dater', but I ignored her, picking up the receiver.

'Hi, Jeremy,' I answered sweetly. 'Oh, a meeting in your

office? Sure. See you in five.'

Becca shook her head as I hurried out of the room, heading to the ladies' to freshen up before my meeting. Perhaps it was best if she did leave. I couldn't stomach the thought of her counselling me 'for my own good' on why I shouldn't be in love with Jeremy Trelawny when I didn't even understand it myself.

*****

I paused outside Jeremy's door, forcing my heartbeat to a slow clip instead of a fast clop. It was always like this when he called me into his office. I'd get myself into a right tizzy. But somehow, I managed to keep my cool when I was in there and talk intelligently with him. At times, I wondered why I put myself through it, but I lived in hope that one day I'd mean more to him than just his senior research assistant.

The problem with the situation, though, was that we worked together. Jeremy's career and reputation at Oxford were too important to him to be involved in an affair with someone he worked closely with, especially if it went pear-shaped. I was hoping that, miracle of miracles, he'd fall in love with me too; and then he wouldn't care about workplace ethics. Until then, I waited in the wings, an understudy, hoping that one day it would be my turn on the main stage.

Today's meeting seemed like it was going to be a short one, and I assumed it was about Becca's resignation. But Jeremy often called me into his office for longer discussions or to have a working lunch so we could converse about my research findings and the statistical data I was gathering for his book. The admiration he bestowed on me when I'd managed to unearth some rare nugget of information to support one of his theories could make me float on air for days. To him, it was probably a throwaway comment. But I relished it, savoured it. Some might call it 'obsessing'. I called it 'cherishing'. Was there even a difference?

Checking for the third time that there weren't any blobs of food on my green silk shirt and smoothing down my black skirt, I rapped on his door.

'Come in, Anna,' intoned Jeremy's deep voice from within, and it sent a light shiver down my spine. I stepped in and shut the door, effectively sealing off the rest of the world, for time always stood still in here. The first impression of entering his office, when he'd interviewed me two years ago, still stuck with me. I'd summarised it into five words so I'd always remember the day we met: wood, paper, glass, warmth, and beauty. Wood-panelled walls, a mess of paper, a lattice picture window looking out onto the quadrangle green, the afternoon sun streaming in, and the man sitting behind the desk.

On this particular Monday morning, the mess of paper had been tidied into neat stacks, the sky was grey through the lattice window, and it could have seemed a little chilly without the sun. But the masculine energy of the man sitting behind the desk warmed the entire room.

Jeremy looked up as I approached. 'Morning. Monday-itis?' he asked.

I sat down in the chair opposite and attempted a more pleasant expression. Dammit, I didn't want him thinking I was a moody cow.

'Morning. Ah, no. I just drank cold coffee. It didn't sit well,' I said.

Jeremy tsked. 'That crap from the kitchen? Can't have my number one researcher drinking bad coffee.'

As I knew he would, he leaned across and flicked on the espresso machine in the alcove next to his desk. Jeremy was a coffee connoisseur and enjoyed trying out different varieties—the stronger the better. I wasn't much of a coffee drinker before I worked with him; now I had a mild coffee addiction. His latest favourite was from El Salvador—a light roast, but potent. It looked like I was going to be wired before lunch.

While the coffee machine cranked and whirred and did its thing, Jeremy smiled at me, and my insides cranked and whirred too. In his late thirties, he was past the bloom of youth, but I thought the faint crinkles at the corners of his piercing blue eyes showed maturity and only added to his attractiveness. To be honest, there wasn't much I didn't like about the way he looked. From his thick chocolate-brown hair to his polished leather loafers and the tight physique in between, it was all good to me.

Jeremy handed me a small white cup of steaming black liquid emitting a rich aroma. He took a tentative sip of his own and licked his lips in appreciation.

'So how's it going with the church records?' he asked, settling back in his chair.

I roused myself, trying not to stare at his luscious mouth like a halfwit.

'Um, good, just a lot of them to get through. Becca's been doing a first scan and handing over anything that needs a deeper look, though I guess I won't be able to rely on her for much longer.'

'She told you about Africa, I take it?'

'She did.'

Jeremy's eyes flicked over my face. 'You're not happy about it.'

I sighed inwardly. There was never much I could get past him. He had a knack of reading my moods. This was why I was worried he'd picked up on my crush. The thought of him finding out how I felt was terrifying.

I took a sip of coffee and blinked as the ensuing blast of caffeine hit my brain like napalm.

'Not really,' I admitted. 'Becca's great. But I can't protest if she's already handed in her resignation and it's what she wants to do.'

'Don't worry, I'll find you another Becca,' said Jeremy breezily. 'I've had twenty applicants already.'

Twenty! 'Wow, the advert was only posted on Friday.'

'Yes, smallpox must be a popular topic,' he replied.

I suspected it was more likely the chance to work with a hot professor.

'Out of curiosity, what's the female-to-male ratio?' I asked.

'Uh ...' Jeremy ran his eyes down his laptop screen, counting under his breath. 'Fifteen female, five male.'

Dammit, just as I thought.

I gulped nervously. 'That ... that's a lot.'

'I know, it's a bit silly. I closed off the job before you came in. There are three main standouts for interviewing to my way of thinking, but I'll let you have a look at them.'

Jeremy swivelled his laptop towards me to display the candidates he'd shortlisted. There were two male and one female. The males I disregarded because as soon as I locked eyes on Lucy Flanagan's CV photo, I knew I was in trouble.

She was Irish with blue eyes, blonde hair, and, judging from the swell of flesh before the photo cut off, an ample bosom.

'I think she's the best of the bunch,' Jeremy said, tapping on the photo of pretty Lucy. My mouth went dry. Seriously? Could this Monday get any worse?

'Her qualifications are top-notch, and she's got excellent references,' he continued. 'But of course, it's up to you since you're the one who'll be working with them closely. I trust your judgement to choose the best candidate, Anna.'

I glowed a little at that and felt relieved. *I have some say in the matter.* I made up my mind there and then. There was no way in hell Irish Lucy would be working in my office!

'OK. Send me through the link, and I'll have a look at them.'

'Excellent,' Jeremy said. 'I'll do that now. Oh, and by the way, the books I requested from the Wellcome Library arrived yesterday afternoon.' He gestured to a sturdy-looking box sitting on the floor by the door. 'I haven't had a chance to go through them yet. Would you mind having a look?'

'Of course,' I replied, eager to help even though it would add considerably to my workload. As well as conducting research for Jeremy's book, I was independently researching and writing a paper on Queen Mary II, who had died of smallpox at age 32.

'We can discuss anything you find over lunch later in the week.'

'Great, I'll look forward to that.' My breath hitched as I realised what I'd said. 'Uh, I mean, the takeaway salads you get from that cafe are delicious. I'll look forward to eating another one.'

Jeremy chuckled. 'Good, aren't they? Anyway, I'd better let you get on with it.' He nodded at the box.

Right. Yes, the books. Our meeting was over. I got up, went over to the box, and hefted it off the floor and into my arms. It weighed a small ton. Awkwardly grasping it against my chest, I managed to open the door, manoeuvre myself and the box through, and inch the door shut with my foot. As it closed, I allowed myself a final tantalising glimpse of Jeremy's handsome face, peering intently at his laptop; he was no doubt checking out Irish Lucy's credentials more thoroughly.

Back in the office, I deposited the box of books on my desk with a thump. Becca glanced over. 'How did it go? You were in there for a while.'

I grunted. 'We were discussing your replacement. But Jeremy said I'd get to choose whoever it is, thank God.'

Becca raised her eyebrows but didn't say anything else, as if sensing that all wasn't well in paradise.

At least I had something interesting to distract me. Unpacking books from an archive was always thrilling. You could practically smell the past seeping from their ancient pages.

Pulling on a pair of white gloves, I cut open the top of the box and removed the foam cushioning material that had been packed in tightly to prevent the books from moving around during transit. There were eight: four small and four large, wrapped in acid-free tissue paper and packed in two layers, spine down to prevent damage to the binding.

I unwrapped one of the small ones first. The cover was dark green and had an intricate gilt-tooled floral border. It was in superb condition, as if it had been someone's treasured possession. But it was the title that instantly caught my eye.

Memories of a Pox-Scarred Maid
by Contessa Mercy Mocenigo

Intriguing. Who was Mercy Mocenigo, and what had happened in her life that was noteworthy enough to warrant writing a memoir? I couldn't wait to find out.

Chapter 2

Chelmsford, 1766

One day, several months after I'd recovered from the pox, my mother told me she was putting an advertisement in *The Chelmsford Chronicle* to offer my services as a housemaid. I was flabbergasted that she would do this to me.

No matter how much I protested, she wasn't to be swayed, and I knew she was desperate for money. With the death of my father, who had been the village blacksmith, we were struggling to make ends meet. Many an evening, my mother cried in the kitchen as she cut up the last of the bread or served my sister and me an apple each for supper. We had some help from the parish, but not enough to feed the three of us. Now I was to be ousted from my house into someone else's to become their maid. And then there was the matter of how I now looked.

I shrunk at the thought of strangers seeing me and pulled my grey shawl tighter round my shoulders. The days were cooler now that summer was over, and it was a relief to have some kind of covering to protect myself from prying eyes—not that I ventured out much anymore.

'Mercy, be grateful that you've had the pox,' said my mother, seeing my action. 'There's many a girl who can't be employed at this time because people think she may bring it into their homes.'

One scant advantage of contracting the pox and surviving was that you were immune to the disease forever after. But this knowledge did little to comfort me, for my life was no longer worth living. I had become a creature to be pitied, avoided, or stared at. Oh, and they did stare and remark.

'That's all very well,' I replied. 'But there are those who won't like to be reminded of it every time they see my face.'

Before the pox, I used to be happy and carefree. But I had become a much-altered girl, one that brooded sullenly on her appearance and who shrunk at the slightest sideways glance. I felt like a monster; and I acted like one—preferring darkened rooms and being alone. My reflection was an enemy that I would try to befriend, but even a slivered glimpse of the crude pockmarks scattered across my cheeks and forehead was enough to sink my heart like a stone.

The pox, though I'd survived it, had scarred me for life. So I didn't feel grateful that I'd had it. I was only sorry I had missed my chance when Death had come calling.

* * *

The advertisement was answered by the rector of Braintree, a small market town just north of us.

Father Sebastian Fannon said in the letter he wrote to my mother that he wished for my services to begin next week. He sounded ancient, and I could only imagine what kind of disarray I would find. I was still quite weak and barely able to keep my own bedroom neat and tidy, let alone clean a whole house.

As my leave-taking grew closer, I tortured myself with thoughts of how Father Fannon and his household would despise me as soon as they saw me.

Too soon for my liking, the day arrived. It was arranged that Mother was to accompany me on the four-hour journey to the rectory and stay overnight to help me settle in. She was then to return to Chelmsford the following day.

My mood that Monday morning was as grey as the early-morning sky. I embraced my younger sister briefly and lifted my small bag into the cart, which was tethered to an impatient horse. The local boy we had hired for the journey was having trouble restraining it from tossing its head about. But once we got moving, it calmed down and clopped steadily down the road with an occasional snort in the brisk autumn air. Summer was well and truly over; and so, it seemed, was my freedom.

We kept a leisurely pace down the narrow country lane, and though it was barely light, I kept my grey shawl fastened tightly round my head so it covered most of my face. It hindered conversation and also served to keep me warm and protect me from the curious glances that we received from the odd passer-by.

Mother tried at first to make conversation about how wonderful it was that I was going into paid employment. But as she would be getting the majority of my wages, I couldn't share the sentiment. Unable to contend with my monosyllabic grunts, she lapsed into silence; and we clopped along, stopping only for a quick lunch of bread and cheese on the roadside.

It was early afternoon when we reached the outskirts of Braintree, and I felt light-headed with fear. I was neither emotionally nor mentally prepared for what lay ahead.

'Well, here we are then,' my mother said brightly, looking around with interest as we passed some small thatched cottages, but they were hardly any different from those in our own town. The dark clouds that had been overhead all morning had dissipated, and I felt the sun warming the top of my head, and my spirits rose somewhat. Perhaps, just perhaps, I would cope.

We clopped through the main street, which was much quieter than Chelmsford's bustle, but I kept my head down anyway. The rectory was the last property of the town, situated away from the main thoroughfare in its own grounds. It was an imposing three-storey red-brick structure with two large bay windows out front and two smaller dormer windows upstairs. A groomed gravel drive, bordered by a carefully clipped box hedge, wound its way up to a black oak front door. Beds of white dahlias bloomed beneath the bay windows.

The place was certainly bigger and grander than I had expected. For my mother also, by the way she was gaping with an open mouth. We had expected Braintree's rectory to be on a par with that of our own modest parish, but it appeared we were wrong. *At least I won't have to worry about getting paid,* I thought.

We got out of the cart and stood there for some minutes before the horse decided it had had enough of us and started wandering off back the way it had come. Since Mother had arranged a lift home with a local farmer, she called out to the boy that she would pay him when she returned. He raised a hand as they ambled off down the road.

As much as I wanted to walk on that nicely raked gravel drive, we found the servants' path and made our way round to the back door. Upon knocking, we were greeted by a kind-faced woman who introduced herself as Margaret, Father Fannon's cook.

She was as all cooks should be: rosy-cheeked, wide-hipped, and displaying a comforting manner which immediately put me at ease. We were bustled into a large airy kitchen with a well-scrubbed wooden table and a black leaded stove.

'Well, my dear, let's have your shawl. It's warm in here, so you shan't have need of it.' Margaret held out her hand and slowly, I unwrapped my shawl and gave it to her. To give her credit, Margaret didn't flinch, but her eyes widened fractionally when she glimpsed my face. We stared at each other for a second, and I thought I saw pity in her expression. But then it was gone, and she smiled broadly at me and hung my shawl on a nearby hook.

'Now then, my dear, would you like to see your room? It's in the attic, but quite comfortable.' I nodded, wondering if I was to be sharing the space.

'You'll be on your own. There are no other servants here but me and a man from the town who comes weekly to do the garden,' she supplied, as if guessing my thoughts. 'The last girl we had left rather suddenly like. So Father Fannon has been doing what he can to keep things tidy, but you know what men are like.' She rolled her eyes. 'Them's idea of cleanliness is not that of a woman's.'

'Is Father Fannon at home?' asked my mother expectantly.

Margaret waved a hand nonchalantly as she hefted my bag with ease up the kitchen staircase leading to the first floor.

'He's off communing with nature as it's fine afternoon but he'll be in shortly to meet you,' she said. 'The back of the house opens out onto a field. So he often takes walks, sketches, or sometimes holds informal Bible studies.'

My mother raised her eyebrows at this, but to me, Father Fannon sounded rather interesting. Perhaps he wasn't an ancient stick-in-the-mud as I had thought.

We reached the top of the stairs, and I saw that an intricately woven carpet runner stretched down the hallway to the main stairwell. My mother remarked on its fineness.

'Oh yes, Father Fannon got that from his trip to Constantinople. 'Twas a mission to send it here, but he insisted on having it,' huffed Margaret as she proceeded up the next flight of stairs.

I lingered behind, seeing a number of framed pictures mounted on the left-hand wall. I looked closer and saw they were pencil sketches of plants and trees. The right-hand side of the hallway was taken up with a series of latticed windows that faced the open field Margaret had described.

I peered through and thought I saw a figure moving

briskly towards a large weeping willow. The glass was so smeared and grubby, though, that I couldn't be sure. I made a mental note to put cleaning the windows at the top of my list of jobs.

My room was up a very narrow winding flight of stairs. Despite being in the attic, it was much brighter and more comfortable than my dark poky room at home, which, although it had been scrubbed thoroughly and all my clothes and bed linen burnt, held unwelcome memories of my sickness.

'This is nice,' said my mother as we looked around. The white-walled room had a sloping ceiling that, had I been taller, would've caused me to constantly duck my head. It was clean but sparsely furnished with a small oak dresser, a hard-backed chair, and a single bed made up with a plain white coverlet dotted with small scarlet roses. *A fitting coverlet for one such as me,* I thought ruefully, bouncing on the bed to test the mattress. It was firm, but not too hard.

I crossed to the window, which looked out onto the gravel path below and beyond to the road. If I kept myself concealed behind the soft blue curtain, I would be able to see anyone who approached the house, and they would not see me.

A door slammed somewhere below in the main part of the house, and Margaret started.

'Lord love us, that'll be Father Fannon come to meet you, and here's me not even with the kettle on. Mrs Graham, you'll be in with me for t'night in my room off the kitchen. Shall we get you settled in down there? Mercy, we'll give you a moment to unpack. Just come down when you're ready. The drawing room's down the hallway from the kitchen, opposite the dining room. The first door on the right.'

I nodded.

'Don't say much, does she?' I heard her comment to my mother as they went out of the room.

My heart was pounding as I left my room and ventured back downstairs to the warm kitchen. I breathed in the aroma of bread, rosemary, and freshly made seed cake. Then rather reluctantly, I set off to find the drawing room. I didn't even know why it was called such a room. *Is this where Father Fannon also does his sketching?* I wondered.

I had changed into my best overskirt and a front-laced bodice of pale green. All had been newly acquired from the local seamstress on credit once my mother knew there'd be money coming in. A matching green velvet ribbon, last year's birthday gift from Father, held back my dark hair. But however much I tried, I knew that my efforts to beautify myself were in vain. I could only hope that Father Fannon, being a man of God, would overlook the distasteful state of my face, for he would have far more opportunity to see it than I would.

I crept into the room so softly that Father Fannon didn't see me at first, and I had the advantage of looking without being looked at. He was talking to my mother in the bay window while Margaret set up the tea on the sideboard.

He was much younger than I had thought, perhaps in his thirties, but only just, and of medium height and slim build. Thick flaxen hair fell in a lock over a broad forehead. He seemed ill at ease in a well-starched rector's outfit with a black waistcoat, breeches, and a white silk cravat tied at his throat.

Margaret noticed me then and beckoned me to help her serve the tea, saying over her shoulder, 'Father, here's Mercy.'

Then before I knew it, my hand was taken in a warm grip, and I found myself staring into an inquisitive pair of green-grey eyes.

'It's a pleasure to make your acquaintance,' said Father Fannon, scanning my face at a closer range than I would've liked.

'How do you do, Father,' I mumbled, dropping an awkward curtsy.

'Oh, she does speak after all,' I heard Margaret say and

chuckle to herself.

'Well, of course she does,' said Father Fannon, helping himself to a slice of seed cake and sprinkling the carpet liberally with crumbs. Margaret subtly handed him a plate.

'Mercy and I will be great friends, won't we, child?' he continued, sitting on the sofa and crossing his legs stiffly. I passed him a cup of tea.

'Er ... yes ... Father,' I said, not too sure about being called 'child' by a man barely out of his twenties. I myself was 18 years old.

'Oh please, call me Sebastian. I can't stand all this "Father" business, though I know Maggie here won't hear of calling me anything else. Thinks she might get struck by lightning otherwise.'

He laughed at this, spraying more crumbs on the carpet. I wondered if I would have to clean them up. Margaret, or should I say Maggie, handed my mother a plate with a piece of cake and gestured to the sofa. Mother looked a bit surprised to be invited to sit with the rector but obediently took her seat next to him.

'Well now, Father, if I may say, it is your title. And who am I to disrespect a man of the cloth?' Maggie said, pouring tea for Mother. Sebastian seemed to find this very funny and guffawed loudly. Luckily, he wasn't chewing on any cake this time.

My mother raised her eyebrows at me as if to say 'Is this man mentally unhinged? Perhaps this was a mistake.'

Indeed, Sebastian seemed unlike any rector I had ever met. When I thought of our own in Chelmsford, with his balding head, spectacles, and habit of sticking his beak into everyone's business, the difference was as chalk to cheese. Sebastian's kindly, relaxed manner was refreshing and I felt relieved that I wasn't going to be scorned as I had feared.

Chapter 3

I shut down my computer and rubbed my aching neck. The light was fading outside. Becca had left half an hour ago. After reading the first chapter of Mercy's book and finding out her last name was Graham, I'd become distracted by the thought of her father and wondered if he'd died of smallpox. It seemed likely since it was highly contagious and she herself had had it. Perhaps her father had cared for her and caught it. Or was it the other way round?

As the mortality data I was compiling happened to include Chelmsford in 1766, I'd spent the rest of the afternoon sifting through the Chelmsford Parish Church records for any mention of Graham. There were numerous smallpox deaths in the months before Mercy left for the rectory and some names so hastily scrawled I could only imagine that the church graveyard was in high demand. I had read several other accounts of mass graves being dug to keep up with the mounting toll of the dead, which made my job harder in trying to find one man as often there was only a first name and a date. But my thoroughness paid off. I found mention of one 'John Graham, blacksmith, PH d 10

June 1766'. 'PH' referred to 'pesthouse', so it looked like I had my answer. Mercy's father had died of smallpox, leaving a widow and two children—one of them who not only had contracted the disease and lived to tell the tale but also had written her tale down.

My mind whirled with the possibility of this rare find—an intimate personal account of a pox survivor! I hoped, as the story progressed, she'd reveal more information about her experience as, up until now, Jeremy's book had been looking rather dry. Mortality stats were all very well, but I knew he was interested in the social impact as well—the psychological effects and the stigma associated with the disease. This woman's insights could add depth and meaning to his text.

Other questions had sprung up as well as I'd discovered from the flyleaf that the book had been printed in Venice. How on earth did a maid from Chelmsford end up a contessa in Venice? And how had she learnt to read and write so well? Literacy rates were lower amongst the English working classes in rural areas, but perhaps she had attended a charity school. It was all a mystery, but one I was eager to solve.

I wrapped the book in the acid-free tissue paper it had come in and placed it, along with a pair of white gloves, carefully in my handbag. Taking a rare book off-site was a big no-no, and I wasn't exactly sure why I didn't just leave it at work and resume reading tomorrow. Perhaps it was Becca's announcement and me being the last to find out or Jeremy ogling Irish Lucy. Something inside me was wanting to rebel. But I couldn't waste time dwelling on my actions. A monthly movie night was being held at my flat, and I had to buy snacks and wine and eat dinner.

Walking down the empty corridor and past Jeremy's office, I wondered if he'd left. Sometimes he worked late, but there was no strip of light under his door, so I assumed he had. Letting myself out of the building's main entrance, I walked down the path, looking up at the pinkening clouds and enjoying the cool air after being inside all day. I rubbed my neck again and felt glad of a relaxing evening ahead with my friends.

Isabel, Eleanor, Lily, and I were diehard Jane Austen fans; and we watched any movie and documentary we could get our hands on. Tonight was the latest remake of *Emma*, which we'd seen three times already. But as Isabel said, 'There are nuances!' I was looking forward to chilling out, eating junk food, and swooning over Regency dresses (and Mr Knightley).

I was about to head through the wrought-iron gate when I caught sight of Jeremy leaning against the bonnet of his car, facing away from me. My pulse elevated, thinking that I might exchange words with him before he drove home. Even a 'Good night, Anna' and a smile would be enough to keep me going, and I could transfer his face onto Mr Knightley's when I was watching the movie. But I heard him call out a greeting to someone approaching from the other direction, and losing my nerve, I backed away and hid behind the nearest bush. A female voice replied, and there was the sound of kissing—whether on cheeks or lips, I couldn't tell. Oh god, he was going on a date. Another one!

I pressed my own lips together tightly and breathed hard through my nose while attempting to see what his date looked like. She must've been a lot shorter than the bush I was currently peering through as I couldn't make her out.

Tentatively, I lifted my head up, trying to see through the branches and over the low stone wall. I made out a pair of slim legs encased in tan stockings and the flurry of a floral skirt whisking into the front seat of Jeremy's black open-top MINI Cooper. The car started up; and the pair of them drove off to indulge in an evening of, I assumed, carnal bliss.

Jeremy had the knack of making women feel special. I knew that very well, and from what I could gather from faculty gossip (Becca) and my own observations (lurking behind bushes), he went on a lot of dates. Was he indeed picky and saving himself for The One or trying to find The

One by dating every woman in Oxford between the ages of 30 and 40?

I was starting to feel like a ridiculous nobody, watching and waiting in the wings. But I couldn't seem to control how I felt about him.

I visited the Sainsbury's near my flat and loaded up a basket with crisps, nuts, and a couple of bottles of rosé. When I got home, I barely had time to heat a fish pie in the microwave, gulp it down, and chuck some crisps in a bowl before the buzzer rang.

'Come up!'

Everyone came piling in the door at once with hugs and kisses. I ushered them through to the lounge while Isabel sorted out the wine and some glasses.

'Is this new?' asked Eleanor, inspecting the side lamp next to the couch. I flushed a little. I'd bought it last Saturday. Poking around in antique stores was now a hobby of mine after Jeremy mentioned one day it was something he liked to do at weekends. But I hadn't bumped into him. Yet. Meanwhile, I figured if I didn't want to look like a pseudo-stalker, I should purchase a few pieces so I could show them to him if he ever came round.

'It's new slash old,' I replied, settling onto the couch. 'I got it at Antiques on High. Cool, isn't it?' The lamp was ornate, having a turquoise decorative base with a delicate flowered shade adorned with amber crystal teardrops.

'Very,' she replied. 'A good find.' Short-haired and brisk-faced, Eleanor was also a history aficionado; she worked in the same building, but in another section researching the Victorian era. We sometimes met up for lunch. I'd invited her along to our monthly evenings as she'd mentioned that she too was a Jane Austen fan, and she'd got on instantly with Isabel and Lily.

'As long as it works OK,' commented Lily, who was on the other side of me, her long legs stretched out on the ottoman. 'You don't want your flat burning down.' Lily was a historical costume maker and often turned up wearing interesting items of clothing. Tonight, she was wearing pale pink lace-up stays over a white T-shirt and a long flowered skirt. With her curly blonde hair and English rose complexion, she looked like a contemporary milkmaid.

'It's fine. It's got a certificate,' I told her, trying not to show my irritation as Eleanor tested the lamp by flicking it on and off.

Isabel, the fourth member of our group, appeared from the kitchen with a tray upon which was an open bottle of rosé, four glasses, a bowl of Wotsits, and another of crisps. She placed it on the ottoman and began pouring the wine while I searched for *Emma* in my list of TV movies.

'Rosé, how civilised,' said Eleanor, leaning forward from her perch on the end of the L-shaped couch and taking some Wotsits. 'I think I'll open one of my cans of cider if you don't mind.' She got up and disappeared into the kitchen.

'After the day I've had, I don't care what it is. I need alcohol,' said Isabel with a sigh.

'Why? What happened?' Lily asked. I was wondering the same thing. Isabel was an art therapist, so it was common for her to have some interesting experiences at work.

'Oh, I've been working with a client going through a break-up. I can't go into details, but let's just say she formed an interesting phallic shape with her clay, and it got thrown violently against the wall.'

I raised my eyebrows at that, and I heard Lily give a muffled snigger.

'Right. Does anyone need the loo? 'Cause I'm pushing play,' I said.

Perhaps I was feeling overly sensitive tonight, but Mr Elton's blatant disregard of Harriet despite her infatuation with him was annoying me. The fact that blonde Emma was reminding me of Irish Lucy wasn't helping.

I squirmed, poured myself another glass of wine, and grumbled under my breath that Mr Elton was a dick.

Eleanor must've heard me as she said loud enough for

the other two to hear, 'Methinks we have Harriet in our midst.' Lily giggled, then smothered it when Isabel, over by the ottoman, looked at her sharply. My gut twisted.

I paused the movie and stared at Eleanor. 'What did you say?' It wasn't like me to be so confrontational, but the rosé was making me bold.

Eleanor shifted uncomfortably. She didn't have a filter at the best of times, and usually, I let her tactless comments slide. But tonight, I wasn't in the mood.

'Nothing. Sorry. Let's keep watching.'

Feeling exposed, I clicked play on the movie, got up, mumbled something about needing to use the loo, and locked myself in the bathroom. Leaning against the sink, I shut my eyes as the familiar burning pain crept over my heart—the pain of unrequited love.

Then came a soft knock at the door. 'Anna? Can I come in?'

Isabel, always the soothing peacemaker.

I unlocked the door, and she came in, her round face sympathetic and her hazel eyes questioning.

'Are you all right?'

I nodded.

'How long have you been in love with your boss?'

I drew a breath. OK, so I was right. They all knew. Becca must've said something to Eleanor. They were on friendly terms and sometimes went to the pub after work, and Eleanor had obviously told the other two. God. I assumed that to them, it was a big joke and I was someone to feel sorry for. Like Harriet in *Emma*, I was a foolish, wretched rabbit.

I didn't really want to talk about it, but Isabel sounded genuinely concerned, and I supposed she dealt with much worse in her line of work.

'Two years, one month, and three days. Pretty much from the day he interviewed me. It was like a lightning bolt zinging from his forehead into mine. And then when he chose me for the job, it felt like it was meant to be.'

'Oh, Anna.'

I sagged against the sink and hung my head. 'I just thought love was meant to feel nicer than this. I didn't count on the anguish and the sleepless nights,' I whispered. *Not to mention the hiding in bushes ...*

Isabel came over and grabbed my hand. 'You should leave and find somewhere else to work. It's obviously torturing you.'

I shook my head. It was too late. I was too far gone on him.

'This is her fault. She Who Must Not Be Named,' said Isabel starchily.

She was talking about my twin sister, Beth, who

currently lived in London with my ex-boyfriend.

'I bet this is a manifestation of what she did.'

'I don't see how.' Though my change of job did happen around the same time so it could be related.

I squeezed Isabel's hand and turned away to run the cold tap, reluctant to talk about my sister.

Splashing some water on my hot face, I patted it dry with a hand towel. 'Don't worry about me. I'll be OK.' After all, as my mother was so fond of reminding me growing up, I was the brainy one. I had the smarts to deal with this. However, like my boyfriend being nicked from underneath my nose, this was a situation not typically found on a school curriculum.

'I know you will,' said Isabel gently. 'Meanwhile, we can try to manage the situation. Why don't you come and do some art therapy on Friday night? I'm running a group session. It might help.'

'OK, maybe.'

The way I was feeling lately, I was willing to try anything.

***

Later that night, after everyone had left, I downed a glass of milk and scoffed a plate of cheese and crackers. The hastily eaten fish pie was a while ago, and the evening's angst had given me an appetite. After I'd come out of the bathroom, no one had said anything, but Lily made me a cup of camomile tea and patted me on the arm. Eleanor had also given me a tight hug and said that we should do lunch tomorrow. I wasn't sure what Isabel had said to them, but I felt marginally better that at least my friends weren't laughing at me behind my back as I feared.

I removed Mercy's book from my handbag and grabbed a pad and pen in case I needed to take notes. Settling down on the couch, I turned on my antique lamp and prepared to work. I knew I'd toss and turn in bed, wondering what Jeremy was up to on his date, so I might as well take my mind off it by doing a few hours of research for his book until I was too tired to think. But working on his book made me think of him anyway!

Chapter 4

Mother left early the next morning after breakfast. We said our goodbyes outside in the cold air and embraced. She urged me to 'work hard and be good'. Then off she went back to Chelmsford with the local farmer on his cart. I felt sad to see her go, but eager to embark on my new life at the rectory now that Sebastian had turned out to be more palatable than the ancient master I had envisioned working for.

When I went back into the warm kitchen, Maggie was fussing over a plump plucked chicken and smearing it with yellow lard. Still feeling hungry, I eyed the bread, butter, and golden honey laid out on the table.

'Have some more, and there's a fresh pot of tea made if you'd like another cup,' said Maggie, flipping the chicken on its back. She didn't have to tell me twice. Plentiful food was a luxury after barely existing. So I ate, drank, and watched as she inserted handfuls of sage and onion stuffing into the chicken and trussed it with twine.

'Father Fannon likes a good roast chicken, he does,

especially one that's been well stuffed,' she said, wiping her hands on her apron and smiling at me. I commented that it seemed like a large chicken for one man to eat all by himself. But Maggie assured me we would be helping him to eat it, and she planned on making soup and a pie with the leftovers. Despite having had a second breakfast, my mouth watered.

After I'd cleared away the breakfast things, my first task that morning was to dust the books in Sebastian's study, which led off from the drawing room. I hadn't noticed any door in the room, but Maggie shooed me out of the kitchen, handing me a duster before I could ask exactly where it was. Sebastian was at church, I assumed.

I went into the drawing room and began searching for the door to the study. After several minutes of aimlessly wandering around and half-heartedly dusting the vases on the sideboard, I came across a black oak door in a small alcove tucked away at the back of the room.

To my amazement, inside was a library room filled floor to ceiling with books. In the middle, surrounded by that literary ocean, was a small writing desk covered with papers and a pot of ink with a quill. Light spilled through a window that had been inset into the bookshelves and a chaise longue in green-and-white-striped silk fitted snugly underneath.

I had never seen so many books. I breathed in that special papery smell that only books seem to exude. As I walked around, my fingertips touched their spines reverently; some seemed fit for kings with rich gold lettering and leather bindings.

One caught my attention more than the others, and I carefully drew it out of the shelf for a closer look. It was a slim volume with a midnight-blue cover and a sprinkling of silver stars on either side of the title. The lettering of the title was also silver and quite long. I touched the letters on the cover expectantly, as if by some miracle, I would be able to read what it said.

'Ah, a fine choice!' a male voice said behind me. 'I've had many a good chuckle at the adventures of Lord Alby and his irreverent escapades.'

I turned, and Sebastian was there, peering over my shoulder.

'Oh!' I said quickly, feeling my face turn red. 'I didn't hear you come in, sir. I was just dusting the books.' But then unable to help myself, I added, 'But, Father—I mean, sir, what is this book called?'

Sebastian took the book from my hand and asked, 'Do you not know, child?'

I shook my head, feeling ashamed. 'No, sir, I cannot read.'

'Well then,' said Sebastian, his green-grey eyes looking into mine intently. 'There's no shame in that, Mercy. Most of my parish cannot read. The book is called *The Mishaps and Misfortunes of My Misspent Youth in Venice*, and it's by Lord Albert P. Ryder—a most delightful scoundrel if ever there was one.'

He went on to tell me that young men, particularly rich ones, go on a grand tour of Europe, where they learn about art and history and other such things and come back enriched and educated by all the sights they have seen. Lord Alby was one such young man who had toured Italy and was so captivated by Venice and all that went on there that he felt compelled to write about it.

'What went on there?' I asked, intrigued. Sebastian shuffled his feet slightly and averted his eyes. I noticed he wasn't wearing his starched black rector's clothing but was in well-cut soft beige breeches and a loose white overshirt with a plunging neckline as one might wear as a nightshirt to bed. He seemed more comfortable in this attire, but it struck me as a strange outfit for a rector to wear. I tried not to look at his chest, which was smooth and slightly pinkish, as if he'd taken a little too much sun.

'Oh, just a bit of nonsense, child. Ahem. But look, I must let you get on with what you were doing. Time's ticking by, and it'll be time for luncheon shortly.' Sebastian handed me the book to insert back on the shelf and walked to the door. By the entrance, he paused and turned to look at me thoughtfully. 'There's not much point having all these books if there's only me to read them. Would you like me to teach you?'

I gaped at him. 'Oh, yes please, sir!' He nodded and smiled softly to himself, then slipped out the door. Inserting Lord Alby's book back into the bookshelf, I resumed dusting. But all the time, I was thinking hard about what Sebastian had said, my heart thudding with expectation.

* * *

My reading lessons began in earnest the next afternoon in Sebastian's study or what I thought of privately as 'the library room'. They continued in the following weeks for an hour each day in the late afternoon when I had finished my duties.

Sometimes Maggie brought in tea and also cake if she had been baking. If she thought anything about my lessons, she kept it to herself, only saying once when she brought in the tea, 'Father Fannon is doing you a great favour, my dear.' Then she pursed her lips and said nothing else about it.

Sebastian's tutoring method was straightforward. Once I

had learnt the letters of the alphabet and their sounds, he read children's stories aloud to me, pointing to each word on the page until I could recognise which words made which sounds. Lo and behold, after a month of stuttering my way through, I could read simple text without too much trouble. He also gave me a small blackboard and a piece of chalk, and I practised writing simple sentences at night in my room until my eyes gave out trying to see by the flickering candle.

During this time, I felt a strange sense of destiny, purpose, and hope all mixed together. Perhaps my life would amount to something and not be ruined, as I was sure it would be, because of the pox. I found myself pondering possibilities and dreaming of things that were quite above my station. Maybe one day I could write a book too. A book like Lord Alby's—an adventurous one! I knew it was wrong, but I could not help it. Sebastian had opened a door in my mind, and there was no going back.

One afternoon, it was quite mild, as if the season had forgotten it was almost winter. Sebastian said he was so pleased with my progress that we should take our books outdoors as there would not be too many more afternoons like this.

Readily, I agreed and ran to the kitchen to collect my shawl; the sun still hurt my eyes and would burn my scarred skin. Wrapping the shawl around my head, I made my way to the old weeping willow in the field at the back of the house.

There was enough heat in the air to feel oppressive, as if a thunderstorm were brewing. It was hot and sticky, and I was glad to reach the cool shade of the willow. Father Fannon poked his head out through the leaves and looked at me.

'Will you not take off your shawl and get some sun, child? It'll be winter soon, and then we'll all be crying out for it.'

I shook my head. 'I'm afraid I can't, Father. The sun burns my face now after ... after my sickness.' I felt suddenly depressed as I remembered why I was now different from everyone else.

'Pah, the pox!' said Sebastian, shaking his head so the willow leaves rustled. 'How I hate the Speckled Monster! This summer, we were luckier than Chelmsford, but we've had our own share of it in Braintree. The year I arrived, people were dropping like flies. It's the most despicable thing I've ever encountered. I myself was inoculated in Constantinople some years ago, so it cannot touch me. But my heart goes out to those afflicted and to those like you, Mercy, struggling to deal with its ... consequences.'

I was surprised to hear him talk so of the pox. I had thought, more fool me, that somehow he had not noticed my pockmarks. So I, for a time, had forgotten them also. But now I knew that he had noticed and felt pity for me. The thought depressed me even further.

Sebastian stretched out a hand slightly, as if to touch my shawl, but then withdrew it. 'Was it ... very bad for you, child? You can tell me.'

I drew a deep breath. Sebastian was the first person I'd met who was willing to lend a sympathetic ear. So hesitatingly, I told him how the doctor had instructed the windows in my room to be shut tight and blankets nailed over them. How it had been turned into a boiling, airless space to contain the infection and sweat the pox out of my body. But this hadn't cured me. It had made the symptoms worse.

'My back felt like hot needles were being poked into it, and my legs were heavy like tree trunks. There was a thick red rash spread across the top of my stomach. Then after a few days, white pustules appeared on my hands. The blisters soon spread to my face and all over my body,' I recounted.

Filled with a watery fluid that then turned yellow, they had left no inch of me spared. Coupled with the horror of turning into a blistered monster, I had felt sorely wretched, like someone had laid me across one of my father's anvils and pierced me all over with a red hot poker.

My mother was too afraid of catching the disease. So it

had been my father, a thick white handkerchief fashioned around his face, who comforted me at night and lifted my head and spooned warm broth down my aching throat during the day. It was also he who changed my bed linen when it was soiled, rolling me gently on my side, despite the doctor giving strict orders that my sheets were infected and mustn't be touched. In my weakened state, I had thought he was an angel come to deliver me from hell.

'After a couple of weeks, the pustules turned into scabs and started falling off. I felt better and could sit up and feed myself,' I told Sebastian, whose face had gone rather pale after hearing all this. 'It was then I knew that I would live. And the doctor, who checked me over when the infection had truly passed, said it was a miracle I hadn't bled within or been left blind.'

'And your father, was he spared?' Sebastian asked.

I shook my head. 'He started having symptoms not long after I recovered and was moved to the pesthouse so as not to infect my mother and sister. But he never came out. That's why my mother advertised my services in the paper. She needed the money.'

'I'm very sorry for your loss, child,' murmured Sebastian as he pressed my hand.

'Thank you, sir,' I said stiffly and turned my head away. The guilt of killing my father pressed upon my chest like a stone, but I didn't want to talk about it with him.

Sebastian must've got my hint as he said, 'Let us talk no more about the pox and look forward to happier times.' Then he lay down on his side in the sun and opened his book. It was 'on philosophy', he told me; and I opened mine, a sweet romance about a boy who bought a cow for his father and fell in love with the hired milkmaid. For a time, we read in silence.

Soon, though, Sebastian started sighing and plucking at his shirt. 'So hot!' I heard him mutter. Eventually, he sat up and pulled the shirt over his head. I was shocked at the sight of his bare chest.

'Sir!' I exclaimed.

He laughed at my horrified tone. 'Apologies, Mercy, but I had to free myself of this cumbersome article of clothing. Rest assured I don't normally go gadding about with my shirt off. Ahem. But I was dying of the heat. You do not mind?'

'Er, no, sir,' I said, not knowing where to look or what to think. I felt like making the sign of the cross but knew he would see and laugh. I tried instead to concentrate on my love story. The boy was helping the milkmaid out in the dairy and they were laughing and having fun as they made butter.

After a time, I sneaked a peek at Sebastian. He appeared

to have dozed off, but then I knew he hadn't as he gave a lazy slap of his hand to his chest to disturb a fly that had happened to land there. I gulped and averted my eyes. As if he felt the weight of my gaze, Sebastian opened one green-grey eye and looked in my direction. 'Have you made the sign of the cross yet, Mercy? I can feel your disapproval burning from here.' He chuckled with amusement.

I said nothing and kept reading about the boy and the milkmaid, thinking that Sebastian, though kind-hearted, was a very odd rector.

Chapter 5

The next morning at work, I was two cups of faculty coffee down and trying to make sense of the pages of scrawled notes I'd taken after reading Mercy's memoir. I agreed with her: Sebastian's shirtless behaviour was unconventional for a rector (and rather entertaining). But he also seemed like a genuinely caring person from what she'd described. Because of him, she'd opened up about her physical experience of contracting the disease and hinted at its emotional impact, which was invaluable information for Jeremy's book. Besides that, the fact that Sebastian had been inoculated in Constantinople was an interesting turn-up.

I knew from my research that before the development of the smallpox vaccine in the late 1700s, the only option for protection from the disease was inoculation. This involved either inhaling highly infectious smallpox scabs or having them put into a small incision in your arm to contract variola minor—a mild form of the disease that wasn't violent enough to kill you. However, if you were unlucky, it turned into the full-blown version, variola major, which could be deadly. Inoculation was common in Europe, Asia, and Africa but considered dangerous in Britain. So Sebastian willingly undergoing this process in a foreign country marked him as a bit of a risk-taker.

But it was also thanks to him that Mercy was able to read and write, and it looked like her desire to write a book had been fulfilled, though I didn't yet know how it had eventuated or why. She'd obviously deemed her stint as a maid adventurous enough to write about in later years. But what else had gone on in the rectory that had compelled her to put quill to paper?

My lunch with Eleanor was at Queen's Lane Coffee House, a fifteen-minute walk from the faculty. Dating back to 1654, it cited itself as the longest-established coffee house in Europe. So for us history girlies, it appealed more than the closer, but run-of-the-mill Caffè Nero. They also did reasonably priced yummy paninis.

Despite my rumbling stomach, I wasn't looking forward to our lunch as I had a feeling I was going to get the hard word about Jeremy. Eleanor was forthright and didn't pull any punches. When she decided you needed to hear the plain truth, the result was searing—like a branding iron on your bum.

When we were settled in our seats (with paninis on the way), I headed her off at the pass by asking about the research she was doing into Victorian slang and its social significance. If I could get her talking about that, I might escape the spotlight.

'It's fascinating. Some of the words and phrases they used back then crack me up. I sit there chuckling away in my corner of the office like a gigglemug.'

'Gigglemug?' I queried.

'Someone who's always smiling or laughing.'

'Ah. What are some other ones?'

'"Enthuzimuzzy". Making fun of someone who's excited about something. Or there's "arf'arf'an'arf". That means "embarrassingly drunk". And I quite like "doing the bear". I might start using that myself.'

I raised my eyebrows. 'Does that mean what I think it means?'

'Depends where your dirty mind's going, young lady. It means "hugging" for your information.'

'Oh, that makes sense. Probably where bear hug comes from.'

We chatted a bit more, but my luck ran out when our paninis arrived. I'd just bitten into my mozzarella, grilled veg, and sundried tomato when Eleanor looked at me. 'So it seems that you're raked fore and aft.'

'What?' I mumbled through my mouthful.

'Desperately in love.'

I ducked my head from her enquiring gaze. 'How do you know?'

'Becca told me.' *I knew it!* 'Anna, I'm going to say something brutally honest. Do you think you can handle it?'

I chewed, nodded, and braced myself.

'I know Jeremy's ripe for a prigging, and I'd be lying if I said my madge doesn't twang when he walks past. But you need to get over him and start dating someone else for your own sanity.'

My lips twitched. Eleanor had obviously been taking in some of the more lewd Victorian slang.

'I don't want anyone else,' I said stubbornly. *Who could compare?*

'You're missing out waiting around for him. You could be feeling the sting of pleasure with someone who does want a relationship with you.'

'Sting of pleasure?'

'Now that does mean what you think it means.' Eleanor waggled her eyebrows, and I laughed.

'I've tried going out on the odd date, but it doesn't make any difference. I don't want to leave my job. So I'm stuck in this ... thing, whether I like it or not.'

Eleanor sighed. 'Look, my cousin, Thomas, is a historical guide. You guys would get on well. He does the Saturday tour at the castle.' She picked her phone off the table and tapped. Next minute, a number appeared in my notifications.

'Oh no. Really, I can't, Nor. Not your cousin.'

'Just have a drink with him. He's single, interesting to talk to, and, no thanks to my aunt's husband, actually attractive.'

I looked at the number and was tempted to delete it, but Eleanor was watching me, steely-eyed.

'OK, I'll think about it,' I conceded.

'Good girl. But please, if you do join giblets with Thomas, I don't want to hear about it.'

'Indeed.'

She didn't have to worry. I had no intention of joining giblets with her cousin in any way, shape, or form.

* * *

It seemed to be the day for unwanted advice and messages. When I got back from lunch, there was an email waiting for me from my mother. It was short, sweet, and to the point: an invite to stay at her flat in London Saturday week. Nothing out of the ordinary. But I knew there was a stinger: my sister and ex-boyfriend would be there.

This was the second time she'd pulled this stunt. She never said specifically that they would be, but there was an underlying current to the message that I could pick up on. I sensed the *intent* of it.

I'd nearly been caught out by the last invitation because I was stressed and thought a catch-up with my mother would be a nice way to unwind. Her three-bedroom flat in Bayswater was an Art Deco escape from reality, and I loved staying there, and sometimes she shouted me afternoon tea at the Park Lounge by Kensington Gardens on Sunday. But due to the terrible weather that weekend and train delays, it was impossible for me to get to London, so I'd had to cancel.

I'd seen her the week after, and she'd said nonchalantly that Beth and Ben had been round for dinner that night and were disappointed not to see me (ugh, their names made me grind my teeth just thinking about them). I said pointedly that they were hardly at the top of my favourite people list and told her to please not invite them round when I was there. She shook her head and replied, 'Life's too short to bear a grudge, Anna. You have to try to forgive Beth for your own sake.'

I said I was doing just fine without forgiving her. Then things got tense, and I left.

Barring another storm or lying to my mother that I was busy, I was going to have to face my sister and my ex. But there was no way I wanted to turn up alone and single and spend an awkward evening fielding pitying looks. I glanced at the Jeremy hotline, wishing I had the confidence and courage to pick up the phone and ask him to come with me. If he were by my side, I'd be able to face it. Perhaps if I couched it as a work favour. But I shrank at the thought. I was too afraid he'd think it was weird or reject me outright. It wasn't as if we were really friends outside of the faculty. And to ask him to travel all the way to London with me was unthinkable. I could fantasise about him whisking me off in his open-top MINI Cooper like one of those women he dated, but I couldn't imagine it happening for real. But who else could I ask?

For the umpteenth time since she'd sent it to me, I looked at Eleanor's cousin's number. She hadn't even told me his last name. I'd added his number to my contacts and labelled it 'Thomas the Tank Engine'.

He didn't sound inspiring.

Becca came into the office, cradling a cup of coffee. 'Just saw your man Jeremy,' she said, sitting down at her desk.

I glanced quickly towards the door to make sure she'd shut it behind her. 'Don't say that!' I hissed. 'He's not my man.'

She pulled a face. 'Sorry, I was only teasing.'

'Well, don't,' I said. Then as curiosity got the better of me, I asked, 'Where did you see him?'

Becca grinned. 'In the kitchen, nicking some biscuits. He asked how you were getting on with the candidates for my job. Apparently, there's someone great who he has his eye on.'

I simmered. *Bloody Irish Lucy!* 'He could've asked me himself.'

She shrugged. 'I guess he didn't want to bother you.'

'Right.'

'So how are you getting on?'

'Oh, OK, I guess. I've narrowed it down to three.'

'Let's see them then.'

Dutifully, I brought up the candidates I'd chosen to shortlist: two studious mousy-haired girls and one thin pale-looking guy—all with distinctions for their master's degrees.

'Which one does Jeremy have his eye on?'

Silently, I brought up Irish Lucy's profile. Becca skimmed her CV along with the CVs of the other three I'd chosen.

'He's right—she is the best one.'

I mashed my lips together. 'I don't want her.'

Becca side-eyed me. 'Are you worried she's going to steal him from under your nose?'

I opened my mouth and shut it again like a goldfish. How could I refute it when it was true? But I had a history of men being stolen from under my nose, and I wasn't willing to risk it again.

'It's not like she's going to be in his office. I never even go in there. You're the one he wants to talk to about his book,' Becca stated reasonably.

'True,' I admitted.

'And if she's as good an assistant as her CV makes her out to be, then you'll be able to focus more on your own research.'

I sighed resignedly. As usual, she was right. 'Fine.' I deleted one of the mousy-haired girls and added Irish Lucy.

'You should probably let Jeremy know so he can set up the interviews,' she remarked sagely.

Grrr. I sent an email to Jeremy telling him my chosen candidates before I could change my mind. If he hired her, she could blooming well do all the boring admin.

A few moments later, I got a reply:

Thanks for that Anna, I'll get onto setting up the interviews. Let's have lunch on Friday and discuss the Wellcome Library books.

The familiar thrill went through me at the thought of spending a whole hour with him exclusively. I supposed I'd better make a start on the other seven books in the box, though I doubted any of them would be as interesting as Mercy's memoir.

Chapter 6

My lessons continued steadily under Sebastian's careful tutelage until I was reading short novels that he let me borrow from his study. I enjoyed the travel stories the most. I'd take them up to my room and devour them by candlelight, thirsty for knowledge of the world outside my own narrow existence.

One night, not long after I'd blown out my candle, I was awoken by an army of wind and rain locked in battle outside my window. First, the wind would howl like a wild animal and shake the windowpanes. Then the rain would splatter against them with a force so considerable that, at times, I thought they surely should shatter.

Underneath this commotion, I fancied I heard the rattle of carriage wheels on the gravel drive. *Surely, there would not be anyone so foolhardy as to venture out in this!* Curiosity got the better of me, and I hopped out of bed and stationed myself behind the blue curtain at the window. Sure enough, directly below was a black carriage complete with a wet stamping horse. As I watched, a figure in a black cloak exited the carriage in the whirling wind, and the thumping noise of the door knocker reverberated through the house.

Maggie will not be pleased to get up! I felt annoyed on her behalf at having to tend to a visitor this time of night (I knew not the hour except that it was very late). For a while, we waited, the visitor and I. There was nothing but the sound of the wind screaming like a banshee round the side of the house, looking for a way in, and the creak of the poplars on the road almost bent double by the force of it.

Then the door was inched open, and a strip of light broke through the darkness. Maggie said something (I couldn't hear what), and the visitor went inside.

She knows them, I thought and felt relief, though I had not realised I was anxious.

Overcome by tiredness, I crept back to bed and fell asleep to the sound of horse hooves stamping on the gravel, thinking, *Someone needs to give that horse some oats. And where will it be sheltered?*

When I awoke the next morning, it was as if the storm had never been. The sky was clear, albeit with the odd scudding cloud here and there. When I looked down from my window, the horse was gone, most likely removed to the large adjoining gardener's shed out the back. But there were debris, branches and leaves, scattered all over the lawn and the white dahlias were now stalks; the wind had guillotined their heads right off.

In the kitchen, Maggie was in a flap, bustling around but not actually doing anything as far as I could see.

'Mercy! Finally,' she said when I walked in. 'We've got an unexpected guest, Mr Donne, Father Fannon's friend. He'll be staying with us while he takes a break from his studies in Oxford. Can you take them's eggs in? I need to pluck the goose for supper.'

My eyes strayed upwards to a bloodied goose dangling by its feet from a hook in the ceiling, its neck crooked. I shuddered.

It wasn't until I had entered the dining room and was walking towards the table that the feeling overcame me. I had felt it before on other occasions, and I always got a little spooked by it. It was as if my body didn't belong to me and that I had walked into this room carrying this tray of eggs a hundred times before. I didn't know what to make of the feeling so I pushed it aside and transferred the heavy tray to the sideboard with some relief.

Sebastian looked up from the book he was reading as I placed the plates on the table and gave me a warm smile. His companion, presumably Mr Donne, was obscured by a newspaper.

'Good morning, Mercy. I trust the storm did not disturb

you last night?'

'Good morning, sir,' I replied, 'yes, it did a little. I heard your visitor arrive.'

'Ah, yes, my friend here has quite the habit of turning up unannounced. Jasper, meet Mercy. She's the clever girl I was telling you about.'

The newspaper lowered, and I just stared. For some cruel trick of fate had placed before me a man that I could never hope to win. And in that split second, when my heart felt like it had been scorched by fire, I wanted to win him very badly. But Jasper Donne was the kind of man who wouldn't look twice at a girl like me or, in fact, any girl of my class notwithstanding her beauty, though I suspected beauty would help somewhat.

He was raven-haired with a wholesome complexion and breathtakingly handsome. Dressed impeccably in a navy silk morning robe with fawn breeches and an embroidered waistcoat, he wore no cravat; and his white ruffled undershirt was open at the throat, revealing a few black hairs.

I saw his perfectly formed mouth moving as he greeted me, and I knew I'd never forget the way he impertinently raked his gaze from the tips of my boots slowly upwards. But when he reached my face and our gazes locked, his scathing dark-brown eyes that were prepared to hold me in so little regard changed, and I saw a flicker of something else.

He shot a glance at Sebastian and said gruffly, 'She's had the pox.' I could do nothing but stand there, my poor pockmarked face turning blotchy with shame.

But Sebastian said (and I'll be forever grateful to him), 'So she has. Not uncommon in these parts, my dear fellow.' Then he took a large bite of poached egg and toast and munched away, unconcerned.

Jasper said nothing else and dismissively returned to his paper. Sebastian gave me a friendly wink, and I dropped a quick curtsy. As I turned to hurry from the room, I noticed Jasper was holding the paper tightly, and his hand was shaking.

I spent the rest of that day in a haze of befuddled thoughts and emotions. I couldn't concentrate on anything. Maggie had to tell me three times to take a saucepan of broth off the stove before it boiled dry that afternoon. I retired to my room soon after, pleading a headache.

The cool quiet of my bedroom soothed my frazzled nerves somewhat, but there was something very wrong with me. *Is this love?* I thought, bewildered. I concluded that it must be but had nothing to compare it against. I loved my family; but it was a love that was quiet and steady, a slow-moving stream that trickled over pebbles, making its way out to sea—nothing like this fire that had torched alight my whole being. Every time I thought of those fathomless brown eyes and sculpted lips, I felt like crying.

Jasper was not only exceedingly handsome; but I had also learnt from Maggie that he was educated, well-travelled, and about to be very rich. He and Sebastian had met in Venice on one of Jasper's grand tours of Europe when Sebastian was taking sabbatical leave.

'Most young men them's have one grand tour,' sniffed Maggie. 'But not Mr Donne—he's had five or six, and him not yet 25 years old! His grandfather is a lord. And once he carks it, Mr Donne will be rolling in it, so Father Fannon says.'

That evening, as Maggie and I were finishing a light supper of cold goose, bread, and watercress soup, the drawing room bell rang. Maggie got up, sighing, her joints creaking. She was soon back, saying that Father Fannon wanted to see me.

I was surprised to be summoned at such a late hour. We never usually communed in the evenings. Nervously, I went into the drawing room; and when I saw that both Sebastian and Jasper were there, my heart started pounding. Keeping my eyes firmly on Sebastian, who was seated on the sofa, I ignored Jasper, who was slouched in the armchair opposite, engrossed in a book.

Sebastian, ever the cordial host, patted the sofa next to him.

'Come and sit down, child. I'm sorry that we missed our lesson this afternoon, but Maggie told me that you weren't feeling well?'

'No, sir,' I replied, sitting on the sofa. 'I had a slight headache, but I am quite well now.'

I stared at Sebastian, terrified that my eyes would stray to those slender, stockinged ankles that were right there at the edge of my vision.

Sebastian grinned and bounced up from the sofa. He disappeared into his study and returned with the book that I had noticed, the midnight-blue one with the silver stars.

'Remember this, Mercy?' he said. 'I think you're ready for it. Some words may be difficult, but just sound them out like I taught you. Lord Alby's Venetian secrets will not be secrets for much longer!'

Jasper still hadn't said so much as a 'good evening', but I could feel his presence was irritated by me. Every so often, a page would turn witheringly. This was proved all too true because as soon as Sebastian finished speaking, he drawled sarcastically from his chair, 'Do you really think that book is suitable, Seb? If the girl must read, surely, it should be something a little more ... maidish.'

I looked at him and immediately wished I hadn't. He'd lowered his book and was sitting there, watching us, his dark eyes glinting, his lips curled in amusement.

'Oh pfft,' said Sebastian, waving his hand dismissively. 'Don't listen to him, Mercy. Jasper thinks women don't have a brain to toss between them, but I disagree. God made men and women to be equal after all.'

Jasper arched an eyebrow and looked me up and down, as if to say there was no way on earth he would ever believe that I was his equal. And I knew it—I knew that what I was doing was wrong and someone of my position should not try to rise above it. But I wanted so much more. So I firmly grasped the book that Sebastian was holding out to me.

'Thank you, Father. I will take it to my room and peruse it before I go to sleep. I will let you know what I think. Good night.' I didn't say 'good night' to Jasper but curtsied to Sebastian and took my leave directly.

As I shut the door, I heard Sebastian say with a laugh, 'That put you in your place, old chap. She's more than meets the eye, that one!'

I heard a gruff reply from Jasper but luckily didn't catch what was said; no doubt it would have been something that would sting and cause me more anxiety!

Chapter 7

Meeting Jeremy for lunch always meant the night before was fraught. I had to block out time for shaving my legs and armpits, body moisturising, face masking, hair washing and conditioning. Not to mention ironing clothes, painting nails, and plucking eyebrows.

By this level of maintenance, you would assume that I was some sort of disgusting hairy beast that had let herself go. I wasn't, and I hadn't. But on 'lunch days', I was spending a longer amount of time in his presence, so I wanted to make sure I was presenting the most perfect version of myself. It was exhausting but worth it in case he happened to have a light bulb moment: *Gosh, Anna is quite pretty*. I could live in hope.

On this Friday morning, though, the unthinkable had occurred. The face mask I'd used last night was a different brand to my usual, and I had applied it liberally. But when I looked in the mirror, I got the shock of my life: there was a huge shiny red zit the size of Krakatoa on my chin! I could've cried after all the effort I'd put in (in fact, I did for five minutes) before toughening up and painting the zit carefully with concealer and powdering the heck out of it. Perhaps if I faced directly towards him, Jeremy wouldn't notice the volcano.

My nerves kicked up a notch as I approached the faculty building. Luckily, the day was cool and breezy, so it had dried my underarms on the fifteen-minute walk from my flat. I *enjoyed* spending a whole hour with Jeremy, but it did mean I needed to reapply my antiperspirant a few times before I even saw him. If I was this much of a wreck being with him for an hour, God knows how I'd ever manage a relationship. But we'd cross that bridge if (when) we came to it. Maybe I'd splash out and Botox my armpits.

Of course it didn't help that Becca, upon catching sight of my face when I walked in, exclaimed, 'Wowser, that's a beauty! Did you eat a whole box of chocolates last night or something?'

I ducked my chin and sidled to my computer, feeling like a swamp hag.

'Aren't you seeing your man today?' she asked.

'For the hundredth time, he's not my man! Haven't you got work to do?' I snapped. That shut her up, and we concentrated in strained silence for the next few hours, only punctuated by Becca's sighs as I sent her a heap of admin emails to deal with.

Maybe I wouldn't miss her as much as I'd initially thought.

The other books from the archive were dry scientific journals written by men and proving time-consuming to get through when I was more interested in Mercy's encounters with Jasper. As much as I hated having a massive zit, at least I didn't have pox scars and had to live in the same house with the guy I had a crush on. From her description, Jasper sounded like trouble, and I had a bad feeling about him— for her sake. It was making me even more jittery as noon approached.

'Come in, Anna,' Jeremy intoned after I'd knocked on his door. I entered, clutching my tablet, prepared to show him the notes I'd made on the books.

He was typing away on his laptop with a serious expression. I stood and gazed, drinking him in. Maybe it was the adorable lock of hair falling over his forehead or him biting his lower lip in concentration. Either way, he was radiating sex appeal. I gulped. Absence had made my heart grow even fonder as I hadn't seen him since Monday.

He waved me over without looking up, and I shook myself from my reverie. As I sat down in the chair opposite, I noticed the paper bag by his left elbow with the cafe logo.

He'd been out to get 'our' salads. That was sweet.

'You like the Caesar chicken, right?' he asked, finally looking up and smiling at me. My chest bloomed. I smiled back.

'Yes, thanks.'

Jeremy's eyes flicked over my face, dropped to my chin, and then he busied himself with taking out the salads. My smile faltered. So much for concealer—he'd noticed the volcano.

'You can eat while I check your notes, if that's OK?' he said, handing me a container and a wooden fork.

'Fine by me,' I said, blushing and hoping my zit hadn't put him off his lamb couscous.

Jeremy reached over for my tablet, and his back gave an almighty crack. He grimaced, straightening up in his chair.

'Gosh, that sounded painful. Are you all right?' I asked.

He tilted his head from side to side, wincing. 'Yes ... just my spine clicking back into place—I had a hard workout last night,' he replied with a rueful chuckle.

I didn't say anything, my mind whirring as the inference sunk in. That sounded awfully like he'd been up all night bonking the woman I saw getting into his car! My fingers tightened around my fork, feeling frustrated and hurt. Without thinking, I said sharply, 'You should stop doing that.'

Jeremy paused mid head tilt, and glanced at me. 'What?'

I coughed and said quickly, 'I mean, you should stop overdoing it at the gym. If you need a chiropractor, let me know. A friend of mine sees a good one.'

'Oh, thanks. I might take you up on that.' He grinned. 'I'm getting too old for these hard workouts.'

I stabbed at a piece of chicken, stuffed it into my mouth, and quietly simmered. *Seriously? What had he been doing with her to put his back out?*

Jeremy rapidly read over my notes and tapped the screen. 'There's not as much information as I thought there would be. And aren't there eight books?'

I swallowed some lettuce. 'Yes, there are. But I'm still going through the eighth one.'

'What is it?'

'Ah, a memoir by a female smallpox survivor who had variola major.'

Jeremy's eyebrows raised. 'Sweet Jesus, really? Does it give much detail?'

'Yes, she recounts her experience of contracting the disease early on in the book.'

'I should definitely read it then.'

I squirmed hearing him say that. If my suspicions were correct about where Mercy's memoir was headed concerning Jasper, I didn't particularly want Jeremy reading it. It was too close to home, and I wanted to protect her (well ... myself).

'That's not necessary,' I said quickly. 'You're so busy with your lecturing, and that's what I'm here for. I'll make sure you have the pertinent bits for your book.' *And leave out anything more sensitive.*

My diversion tactic worked. Jeremy nodded. 'OK, that might be best. I have got a full schedule at the moment.'

He passed my tablet back, glanced at me, and, pointing at his chin, said, 'Ah, you might want to ...'

I dabbed at my chin with a napkin, thinking I had dripped mayo on it. But when it came away soaked in watery pus, I realised in horror—the volcano had erupted!

***

Isabel clapped her hands loudly, and I jumped. By the surprised looks on the faces of the other women around the table, I wasn't the only one who had been startled. I didn't realise my easy-going friend ran such a tight ship. Then again, this was the first time I'd been to her art therapy class at the community centre, and people were always different in a work environment.

After the disastrous pimple-exploding incident in Jeremy's office, I'd slunk to the ladies' and had a self-pitying sob in a cubicle about the sorry state of my life. In desperation, I'd messaged Isabel, and she'd fitted me into the class after work. So far, it had been drinking cups of tea and eating biscuits, but it appeared we were about to get down to business.

'Right, ladies,' she said in a no-nonsense tone as the chatter ceased. 'Let's get started. You each have a ball of clay that you're free to mould into whatever shape you please. But the object you make should represent the person who has hurt you and encompass your pain. There are various tools in the jars if you need them for rolling, cutting, and texturing.'

A woman tentatively raised her hand. 'Does what we create have to look ... good?'

Isabel shook her head. 'As long as you know what the object represents, it doesn't have to look professional. I'm not expecting any budding Michelangelas.'

A few women tittered at that. 'Don't you mean Michelangelos?' asked one.

'No,' said Isabella firmly. 'This is a man-free zone. In here, it's women only.'

Wow, OK, this could be interesting. I didn't realise she was such a staunch feminist.

Isabel tapped at her iPhone. 'You have half an hour to create your object. I've set the timer. Go!'

There was an instant flurry as the other women started moulding their clay balls or tearing off smaller pieces and shaping them.

My own grey sphere sat in front of me, and I prodded it, feeling hugely uninspired. What could I create that encompassed my pain? Jeremy and his latest date bonking? That would take a lot longer than half an hour, and I definitely needed Michelangela skills for that. Maybe I could poke a hole in it with a stick and say it represented my painful zit.

I side-eyed the woman next to me to see what she was making. She was busily rolling a sausage shape and had two smaller balls already made. The woman next to her was also making a clay penis. Oh well, if you can't beat 'em ...

'Time's up, ladies!' Isabel shouted, and I almost leapt out of my skin since she was standing right next to me. She strode around the table, peering over people's shoulders—nodding, commenting, and sometimes raising her eyebrows. I hoped I wouldn't have to do a show-and-tell as to whose penis I'd created and why it had caused me pain. But I was quite pleased with my creation, to be honest. I'd even done some detailing to make it look more authentic. Not that I knew what Jeremy's penis looked like, but since the man was an Adonis, I'd tried to do his nether regions justice.

'Very nice, Anna. One of the best I've seen, and there are quite a few specimens here,' remarked Isabel as she reached the head of the table again, and I felt smug for creating a top-notch clay penis.

That was me, though, such a goody-goody—always doing extra homework to receive praise from my teachers at school, coming home with certificates and awards to bask in even more praise from my mother.

'Anna's the brainy one, and Beth is the pretty one,' she'd tell her friends, as if both traits were equally as important. I guess in the patriarchal society we live in, she wasn't too far wrong. But the fact that we were identical twins also made it kind of confusing.

'OK, ladies, now I want you to focus on your object and channel all your pain and heartbreak into it,' said Isabel. 'Go on,' she encouraged as she saw us hesitating. 'This is the prick that's making your life hell.'

I glowered at my clay penis, imagining Jeremy dancing about naked, waving it in front of my face, and taunting me, *See this, Anna? You're never going to have it. Because I only go out with pretty girls, not brainy ones. I'm going to call you into my office and sit there looking beautiful with this gorgeous member between my legs and make you suffer.*

I felt rather silly thinking this, but all the other women were frowning and muttering at their clay, so I didn't feel too weird.

'Good work, everyone. Now under the desk is a shelf, and I want you to bring out the tool you'll find there.'

Curiously, I reached underneath and gripped a smooth rubber handle. Bringing it up to table level, I saw it was a small but strong little hammer. I wasn't sure why Isabel didn't place them on the table. Dramatic effect?

'Right, ladies,' she said, beaming. 'This is the therapy bit. I want you to pound the living daylights out of your object.'

I blinked and glanced around. The other women were grasping their hammers and looking uncertain too.

'Aren't we going to get them fired?' asked one. 'I spent ages doing the pubic hair.'

'The only fire that clay penis is going to feel is the heat of your anger. What are you waiting for? Pound!'

Obediently, we tapped our clay creations timidly.

'Harder!' exclaimed Isabel excitedly. 'Feel the rage!'

Somehow, her encouragement infected us; and we started wildly smashing our hammers, obliterating our creations to smithereens. The noise was incredible. Some women were screaming. Others were crying. Some (like me) were giggling uncontrollably. Bits of wet clay flew into the air, and I felt it land in my hair and stick to my face. I'm pretty sure I also breathed some in.

After a few minutes of everyone letting loose their

emotions, Isabel clapped her hands, and the banging ceased. 'Now for some feedback. How did that make you feel?' She looked around the table and clocked me. 'Anna?'

Breathing hard, I looked down at Jeremy's make-believe penis, which was now a flattened pulpy mess. No way he was using that anytime soon. He'd need corrective surgery. I spat a bit of clay out of my mouth and grinned at Isabel.

'Strangely satisfying.'

*****

Buoyed by the adrenaline rush I'd experienced at the art therapy class, I immediately went home and replied to my mother, telling her I'd come and stay next Saturday. Then I booked a ticket for an Oxford Castle & Prison tour tomorrow. It felt good to take action rather than being a passive observer.

But being a passive observer on the tour was what I needed to be. My plan was to check out Eleanor's cousin, Thomas, incognito and see what he was like. That entailed wearing inconspicuous clothing: a grey sweatshirt, black leggings, ratty old trainers, and a cap. Plus lurking at the back of the group, not asking questions, and generally avoiding suspicion. I was pretty sure Thomas had no idea who I was, but I wasn't taking any chances. Eleanor may have mentioned me and shown him a Facebook photo.

However, I wished she had shown me a Facebook photo of *him*. I'd had a bit of a madge-twang moment when the tour started. She'd mentioned he was attractive, but I hadn't counted on Thomas being quite so good-looking, and it had thrown me a bit. Short dark-blond hair that was longer and tousled on top, a hint of stubble, and a pair of intelligent brown eyes. He was medium height, and I could tell there was a decent body under the white prison garb he was wearing too. Plus he seemed kind of cool and personable, judging by the way he held everyone's attention. Intrigued, I crept forward when we were in one of the dungeon rooms so I could hear better.

He was recounting a story about a woman called Mary Blandy, who had been imprisoned and hanged for poisoning her father. 'It's not entirely clear what happened,' said Thomas, gazing around at the group. 'Mary was a well-educated and respectable young woman. But she met Captain William Cranstoun, who was already married, and he made a play for her.'

Humph, typical, I thought and inched forward until I was near the front of the group.

'He proposed but kept stalling, trying to annul his previous marriage, and Mary's father became suspicious. William sent Mary what he said was a "love potion" and asked her to add it to her father's food so he'd be more amenable to their relationship. Unfortunately, it contained arsenic, and her father died. Mary was imprisoned here for the crime of parricide. She was hanged on Easter Monday, 6 April 1752.'

Unable to help myself, I remarked, 'It sounds like Mary was a scapegoat. Why did William get off scot-free? They should've hung *him*.' A few of the women in the group murmured in agreement.

Thomas smiled amiably, his eyes sweeping my face. 'Well, she wasn't that innocent. The jury went through all the evidence—'

'But that was probably made up of men. Of course they were going to be on William's side,' I interrupted.

'That's a valid point,' said Thomas, casually leaning against the wall of the cell. 'Her case was debated for years afterwards, and in the nineteenth century, it was re-examined more sympathetically. Many believed she was wrongly accused and just a "poor lovesick girl".' He used air quotes.

'Well, there you go ...' I began, ready to make some more pointed remarks on Mary's behalf, but Thomas cut me off before I could.

'If you like, we can discuss it more after the tour,' he said politely with a wink. 'Let's move on, shall we? We've got some more rooms to visit.'

I shuffled after the group, kicking myself for opening my mouth. Now Thomas definitely had me on his radar. He kept staring at me with a mulish expression whenever he said anything, probably thinking I was going to start a feminist rant.

When he told us about a 7-year-old orphan girl who had been imprisoned during the Victorian era for stealing a pram and sentenced to hard labour, I thought I might. But I kept quiet even though I felt like saying something cutting about the injustice of it. Isabel's session last night had really fired me up.

At the end of the tour, we were able to explore the prison at our leisure, so I peeled off from the group and wandered back the way we'd come. I wanted to examine the 900-year-old crypt underneath St George's Tower again. There were some engravings on the pillars holding up the arched roof that I hadn't had a chance to look at during the tour.

I thought I was on my own in the cold, dimly lit space, but a deep voice said, 'Did you know this is the most haunted space in Oxford?' I almost had a heart attack. As Thomas emerged from the darkness with a 'wooo' noise and wiggling his fingers, I frowned.

'Oh, it's you,' I said.

Thomas smiled. 'Just me,' he replied genially, and I

relaxed. There was something about his manner that made it difficult to be uppity with him.

'Who's it haunted by then?' I asked.

'Brother Bernard, the drunken monk, apparently.'

I snorted. 'Have you seen him?'

'No, never. But then again, I'm pretty oblivious about stuff like that. Probably a good thing since I'm down here a lot,' he said.

'Yes, probably,' I agreed.

He threw me a quick glance. 'So what's your deal? You seem like you know some stuff by the way you were challenging me about poor Mary back there.'

'Challenging' him? I simply had a differing opinion to the history books.

'I'm a historic researcher,' I replied a bit defensively.

'Ah, makes sense. Are you at the faculty over in George Street?'

I nodded warily.

'My cousin works there. Do you know Eleanor Jackson?'

I couldn't lie. 'Yes, I do.'

Thomas gave me the once-over, taking in my cap and dowdy sweatshirt. I could see the wheels turning in his head. Damn, he wasn't stupid. And he was hot. No wonder Eleanor was offering him up as a distraction from Jeremy.

I started edging towards the passageway. 'Anyway, I

should get going.'

'Yeah, I'm off too. After you,' he said, waving me in front of him.

I trotted along in silence with Thomas practically breathing down my neck but when we reached the entrance, he jumped in front to open the door.

As I stood in the courtyard, blinking in the late-afternoon sunlight, Thomas materialised beside me.

'So I'm heading to the pub. Did you want to come with?'

I tensed. He'd obviously put two and two together and realised that I'd booked onto the tour to suss him out. How embarrassing!

But what did I have planned? A trip to Sainsbury's for a bottle of wine and a heat-and-eat meal for one, then an evening alone in front of the telly.

I shrugged, attempting to seem casual when, really, I'd been sprung like a jack-in-the-box. 'I guess so. But I'm not dressed to go out, and you might want to change?'

'Nah, they're used to me at the local.'

So much for being incognito. I was now on a quasi-date with a guy who looked like he'd escaped from a nineteenth-century prison!

Chapter 8

If this was love, I didn't think much of it. Mostly, it was misery shot through with rays of heaven when I happened to glimpse a starched elbow from a doorway, a tuft of raven hair outside a window heading towards the makeshift stables, or a well-polished boot travelling past the kitchen door.

My days continued as usual, but Jasper was always on the edge of my consciousness, like an itch I couldn't scratch. I could not help but think of him in the morning when I tidied away the breakfast things and saw the cup from which he had drunk. Or in the afternoon when I saw a book he'd been reading left spreadeagled on the sofa. Then again in the evening when I smelt his strange and exotic cigar smoke waft through the house.

He invaded the very air I breathed. I felt his presence drifting through the house like spores from a dandelion, but I couldn't get a hold of my mind whenever I was in the same room as him. My vision seemed cloudy and smeared, as though I was peering at him through the upstairs windows, which still needed a good clean.

Throughout the next week, he didn't speak to me other than a forced 'thank you' whenever I cleared his plate or poured his coffee. This was not too surprising seeing as I was a servant, and Jasper had classed me with the lowliest of worms. I saw him wince each time Sebastian addressed a friendly comment to me and my ensuing reply was not in keeping with my position.

When I reported back to Sebastian about Lord Alby's book (I had read it over three nights and found it entertaining, if a bit lewd), I could see it pained Jasper dreadfully. 'Why are you teaching her to read?' his grimaces seemed to say. 'She is a housemaid and will stay that way. Why make her think she is anything else?'

As I could not gain his admiration, I took my pleasure from looking at him instead. I learnt to observe without seeming to do so. With a quick eye swivel while putting down the rack of toast, I could see he looked tired. Did that annoying rooster wake him at four o'clock this morning as it had done I? Or a downwards glance while pouring coffee would show me his nails were bitten ragged. Was he nervous about something? If I stood slightly closer (but not too close!) on the pretence of brushing away crumbs from the tablecloth, I could inhale his subtle odour of spice and smoke.

I yearned for there to be some sign that he was similarly affected. Apart from his hand shaking while clutching the newspaper the first evening, I had never seen him anything but composed. He seemed to have a ready wit, although at times bordering on the sarcastic; and Sebastian enjoyed his company, even if for the sport of goading him about his airs and graces. In fact, half the time, I don't think he even knew he was being goaded as he refused to believe that anyone else's opinion could be superior to his own.

It was strange, but Jasper's shortcomings only served to make me desire him even more. I could see what he was, but I loved his imperfections nonetheless. The unbearable sting of some pompous comment was conjured like magic into a sweet rush of affection by my forgiving nature. The curl of a disdainful lip transformed into an adorable quirk and a contemptuous eyebrow arch could almost make me swoon.

Until now, I had held myself to be a sound judge of character. When one's face is marked by the pox, you can easily see through people who don't wish to delve deeper than the ugly casing. I knew Jasper to be one of them, but it was like he had me under a kind of spell, and it was bewildering. I had never experienced anything like it before.

My one fear—and it was my greatest—was that he would somehow discover how I felt. I sensed keenly that this knowledge in his hands would not be a good thing. So I strove to keep my feelings hidden at all cost—and I almost succeeded.

As requested by Sebastian, one of my tasks was to clean Jasper's room. This usually took place when Sebastian knew that Jasper would be out of the house for a certain period.

The first time, I merely changed the sheets on the bed and gave the dresser a cursory dust. But this time, when Sebastian requested it, I leapt at the chance. Snooping wasn't in my nature, but I knew that this would be the only way to find out anything about Jasper as I couldn't ask too many questions of Maggie.

Everything I knew about him I could count on the fingers of my left hand, and such was the disastrous state of my heart that the merest drop of knowledge could quench its thirst for days.

On this occasion, Jasper left the house after breakfast to go riding, so I hurried up the kitchen stairs and along the corridor to his room, fearful that he could return at any moment and find me in there. The room was in some disarray. Piles of clothes were on the floor, so it took me a while to search the pockets of his breeches and waistcoats thoroughly for any letters or trinkets. I found nothing but a few acorns.

After tidying the clothes, I turned my attention to his

dresser and slowly slid out the top drawer with a beating heart. But the contents didn't tell me much: a pile of handkerchiefs, a bit of loose change, and a Bible, which I'm sure was probably Sebastian's. The bottom drawer was empty. I was growing frustrated. Jasper must have some personal keepsake or letter that would reveal something—anything.

Then horror of horrors, I heard footsteps on the landing outside heading directly for the room! Without thinking, I threw myself into the armoire and had just pulled the door shut when Jasper strode in. The door was solid oak, so all I could hear was muffled footsteps walking deeper into the room and then stopping. I was sure he could hear the pounding of my heart—it was so loud. *Dear God,* I prayed, *whatever it is he's come back for, please don't let it be in the armoire!*

In the darkness, I shut my eyes and kept very still. I didn't hear Jasper take another step. The tension was unbearable, and I hardly dared breathe. I grasped a nearby coat for comfort and reached my hand inside its depths. My fingers touched paper in the breast pocket. A letter! Slowly and unbelieving of my daring, I slid it from the coat and deposited it into my apron. I wondered what on earth I was going to do with it, but I tried not to think about that.

Jasper let out a sigh of exasperation, then walked

abruptly to the dresser, and I heard a drawer being yanked open and coins jingling. Then he left. I felt like collapsing and never coming out of the armoire, but I had to. I waited for what felt like ten minutes, then waited another five for good measure. By this time, I was utterly fed up with the armoire and the scent of camphor from Jasper's coats was making me feel light-headed.

Cautiously, I creaked open the door and peeked out. Empty. I crept out softly and tiptoed across the room. When I reached the dresser, I spied something that nearly made me pass out: my dusting cloth was on the floor by the bed. I felt physically ill knowing he must have seen it. Hoping he thought it was Maggie's, I stuffed it into my apron along with the letter and left the room with some relief.

Jasper was outside, leaning casually against the main stair banister, and he looked at me quizzically. We stared at each other. I didn't know for the life of me what to say. The silence became thick and awkward. His eyes bored into me until I felt like a moth pinned to paper. A slow blush started at my neck and moved upwards until I was squirming with embarrassment. Jasper's eyes narrowed as he noted my extreme discomfort at being caught out.

Then my worst nightmare happened; something clicked into place in his head. I could almost hear the pieces of the puzzle lock together. And then he smiled—a slow devastating smile that made me fear he knew the thing I had most wanted him not to find out. Still smiling, he tossed a coin in the air, caught it, and walked off down the stairs, leaving me gasping in despair. I knew I was in big trouble.

For the rest of the day, I was in a state of agitation. I had managed to govern my senses somewhat where Jasper was concerned. But now I completely lost control of my mind, and it spun wildly in a universe of its own. All I could think was *He knows I'm in love with him. Dear God, what is he going to do?*

Maggie saw my edginess and commented, 'Lord love us, girl, you're out of sorts today. That's the third time I've asked you to pick basil, and you've brought me back parsley. What's with you?'

I made some excuse about feeling poorly and escaped as soon as I could to my room late in the afternoon. I stood by the window, took some deep breaths, and leaned my hot forehead against the pane. I had to leave the rectory. I couldn't continue to work here now that Jasper had this kind of control over me. I was under no illusion the feelings would be returned. How could they be? There was no way I—a poor pockmarked housemaid—could compare to the kind of rich, beautiful women he would love and admire.

Feeling sick to my stomach, I undressed and went to bed.

I soon fell into a restless sleep, and my dreams followed suit. I found myself outside a closed door, which I couldn't open no matter how much I tried. In desperation, I kicked it angrily, and it yielded. Inside was a bed in disarray, and I started to tidy and straighten the bedclothes. But when I reached under the covers, a cool hand grasped my wrist and pulled me down into the darkness. I could feel warm breath on my face and hands on my waist.

'No!' I cried and twisted to get away.

'Mercy, it's me,' said Jasper's voice in my ear, and I instantly stopped struggling. The darkness gave way to light, and I saw that it was indeed him. A red sheet was draped around his body. Our faces were so close I could see each individual eyelash framing his liquid brown eyes.

When I looked down, I saw that I no longer had pox scars on my arms and hands; and when I touched my face, it was smooth and unblemished. Tears of relief leaked out of my eyes. To be with Jasper like this and be disfigured would be unbearable.

'I never realised you were so beautiful,' he said and traced a finger down the curve of my cheek. His other hand stroked down my hip, and my body swam with desire.

'Do you think I am too?' He pushed away the sheet covering him, and I gasped in horror at the deep-pitted scars scattered all over his chest.

'No!' I cried. 'I want you to be perfect! I thought you were perfect!'

'What you see is what you get,' he said mockingly and tried to press up against me. I recoiled in disgust.

But Jasper laughed, grabbed my head, and tried to kiss me with lips blistered with pox pustules. I screamed with some force, and this woke me up. I lay there in the darkness, sweaty and shaking. The dream was so upsetting to me that I cried for some time and wondered what it could mean.

I knew one thing for sure: the next time Sebastian wanted me to clean Jasper's room, I would ask Maggie to do it.

Chapter 9

'What would you like, Anna?' asked Thomas when we arrived at the Castle, a black-and-white Tudor-style pub a couple of minutes' walk from the castle proper.

'Oh, I can get mine. Don't worry,' I said, feeling weird about him paying for my drink. I'd formally introduced myself on the walk over, thinking that I'd better since he didn't actually know my name.

'It's not a problem,' he said, trying to catch the barman's eye. 'I get paid prison wages.'

He seemed adamant, and I didn't want to be rude. 'OK, I'll have a cider, thanks.'

The barman came over and greeted Thomas with a 'Hey, mate'. So I gathered he did come here quite a bit. As he ordered for us, I looked around at the pub. It was rustic with an eclectic mix of wooden tables and chairs and not too busy since it was late afternoon. I'd never been here before despite living in Oxford for the past five years.

Thomas nodded towards one of the booth seats and carried the drinks as I slid in. Now what? Make small talk? I wasn't good at that at the best of times. If I knew I was going out with a guy, I needed at least a week to prepare my body and my outfit. I couldn't just be spontaneous. But I got the impression Thomas, now sipping from his Pilsner across from me, was taking this in his stride. He seemed like a casual kind of person. I took a large swallow of cider to help calm my nerves and attempted to look natural as if I went out with strange men all the time.

'Ah, that's better.' Thomas leaned back and stretched out his legs, being careful not to knock my ankles. 'Saturdays are always hectic, but I did sign up for weekend tours, so I shouldn't complain.'

'Are you a full-time tour guide?' I asked politely.

'No, part-time. I manage an e-bike shop during the week and on Sundays.'

'Oh.' I thought this over. 'So do you work at the shop, or do you actually own it?'

Thomas's mouth quirked. 'I actually own it. Are you into biking? I could probably do you a deal since you're friends with Eleanor.'

'Oh, not really, but thanks.' Eleanor didn't mention anything to me about him owning a business. I peeked at Thomas through my lashes when I took another sip of cider. *She also didn't mention he had a cheeky grin, warm brown eyes, and sex appeal. But then again, why would she?* I felt a bit silly for putting him in my phone as 'Thomas the Tank Engine'.

'So how did you get the gig at the castle?' I asked.

'I did a double degree in history and economics,' he said

as if that explained it. 'Hey, shall we get some loaded fries to share? I'm starved. Unless you want a burger? They do vegan ones.'

'Why do you think I wouldn't want a meat one?'

'I figured you might be into plant-based food,' he said with a small smile. 'You seem the conscientious type— someone who likes to do their bit for the planet and check out men before she goes on dates with them.'

I flushed. Dammit.

'Fine. Yes, I would like a vegan burger, but only if we split the bill.'

'Sure. I'll order and get another round of drinks then.'

He sauntered off towards the bar, and I relaxed. So this was a proper date since he'd labelled it as such! Maybe that's what I needed: to be caught off guard, herded to a pub, and fed a vegan burger. If this had been formally arranged by text, I would've been a nervous wreck worrying about every minor detail. But here I was, dressed like a homey with a zit on my chin, and Thomas didn't seem to care less. But then again, he wasn't Jeremy, so I had less skin in the game. Going out to dinner with *him* would be a monumental event, but dreams were free.

We'd eaten our burgers and were on the fourth round of drinks, my shout. The pub had filled up considerably, but it was getting on for eight. I was enjoying this date way more than I thought I would. Thomas had pushed up the sleeves of his prison shirt to reveal extremely muscular forearms, which were quite distracting. As well as telling me more about the e-bike shop, which he'd started with savings from a couple of years working as an investment banker, he'd been regaling me with funny stories about guiding at the castle.

Somehow, we got back onto the subject of Mary Blandy. Thomas mentioned she'd had smallpox and her face was badly scarred. So her father had offered a substantial dowry to entice eligible gentlemen to marry her. I was adamant that her dowry was instrumental in Captain William making a play for her and utterly convinced she had been wrongly hanged.

'Mary's story could be added to the book. She had smallpox, and the dates are right,' I mused, playing with the end of my ponytail. I'd ditched the cap and tied my hair back hastily and hadn't even been to the bathroom to check if it was neat and tidy. This level of nonchalance was unheard-of for me. Though slightly fuzzy-headed after four ciders, I was still coherent—and definitely not drunk!

'What book?' Thomas's foot nudged mine under the table, but I didn't mind. He'd been doing that on and off for the last half hour.

'I'm working on a smallpox project being undertaken by my boss, Professor Trelawny—Jeremy. He's writing a book.' My stomach fluttered a bit upon saying his name aloud. God, what was I like?

'Wow, he's quite famous in history circles.' Thomas raised an eyebrow and looked impressed. 'What's it like working for him?'

Sublime hell, I thought. 'Great,' I replied a tad too enthusiastically. 'He trusts me to take the initiative. We have weekly meetings, and he makes us fancy espresso. He's turning me into a bit of a coffee connoisseur ...'

I could hear my voice taking on that wistful, dreamy tone, and I flushed. Thomas's gaze was assessing, and I averted my eyes, feeling exposed. 'I should probably get going. I think I've had one too many. But it's been nice chatting.' *And I could report back to Eleanor that I had gone on a date with him.*

'Yeah, we should do it again,' said Thomas unexpectedly.

'Really?' I had thought it would be one and done.

'Sure. I had a good time. You're interesting to talk to since you're a history nut too.'

I giggled. 'I've never thought of myself as a history nut, but I guess I am.'

'I'll walk you out.'

'OK.' I stood up and swayed slightly like I was on a full-rigged ship at sea.

'Whoa, easy.' Thomas grabbed my arm, and we staggered out of the pub. Maybe it had been five ciders. I'd lost count …

Outside, I gulped in some mouthfuls of fresh night air, and my head felt slightly clearer.

'Thanks. I'm not used to drinking that much,' I said, disentangling my arm from Thomas's. 'Only the odd glass of wine at our Jane Austen evenings.'

'Oh, I think Eleanor mentioned that. Sounds like fun.'

'Yes!' We walked down the street together, chatting about Jane Austen, of whom I discovered Thomas was a fan, until I realised I'd just been going along with him and we'd crossed over the river.

I stopped walking. 'I'm going in completely the wrong direction!' I poked his shoulder. 'You've been distracting me with *Pride and Prejudice*.'

Thomas laughed. 'Where are you supposed to go, my fair lady?'

'Back yonder.' I waved a hand in the general direction of my flat.

'Come to mine for a coffee if you want. I'm literally five minutes from here. You can sober up and tell me all about your Mr Darcy fantasies.'

I wavered. I should go home and read some more of Mercy's memoir. I was dying to find out what happened with her and Jasper. But the night was still young, and he did want to discuss Mr Darcy ...

Thomas lived in St Thomas's Street. When I found that out, it tickled me so much that I giggled with glee and whacked his elbow. Unfortunately, this caused his key to go flying out of his hand and into the bushes of a neighbour's front garden. He had to go crawling around in there on his hands and knees, which made me giggle harder.

'Stop laughing. You'll wake them up!' he hissed.

'It's only eight thirty!'

'They might have babies or something.'

'Do they?' I whispered.

'How the hell do I know? I never talk to them.' I pressed my lips together to stifle another giggle. There was the sound of rustling leaves, and Thomas backed out of the bush with the keys dangling from his mouth, growling like a dog.

I cackled like a crone.

We lurched down the street and into his flat with me stating that I couldn't stay for long as I had important work to do.

Then somehow, after the kettle had boiled and cups of

instant coffee were made, we ended up in his bedroom, sitting on his hastily made bed. The hot coffee (Sainsbury's Gold Roast) definitely sobered me up, and I realised that (*a*) Thomas kept glancing at me in a certain way and (*b*) I didn't mind it. That, in fact, I was glancing at him in a certain way too.

Depositing my empty cup on the bedside table, I suddenly felt shy.

'Um, we could lie down for a bit. Only if you want to,' he suggested.

I gulped. 'OK.'

'Sorry, the bed's not made. I wasn't expecting a guest. Hang on.' He hastily plumped the pillows, yanked the cover smooth (with me sitting on it), switched off the main light, and turned on a nearby lava lamp—all in the space of ten seconds flat. I blinked at the transformation from ordinary room to amorous boudoir.

Then Thomas did something that shocked me. He removed his white prison uniform shirt and trousers, then his blue T-shirt and boxer briefs. Then seemingly unconcerned that he was stark naked, he hopped under the duvet.

I sat there feeling a bit stunned at having seen his bits, albeit a five-second flash. Apparently, 'lie down' in his book meant 'horizontal nakedness'.

'Are you getting in?' he asked from the depths of the duvet.

'Um.'

I had no intention of revealing my body—even if it had been recently shaved, moisturised, and plucked—to a guy I'd just met. The best thing to do, I decided, was to get under the covers fully clothed, minus my ratty trainers and the cap. It was either that or run away screaming.

'OK, so now I feel a little underdressed,' said Thomas, sounding amused as I wiggled my way in and lay on my back.

'When you invited me over for coffee, I wasn't expecting us to get naked,' I replied, very aware of the heat radiating from his body only centimetres away. 'Do you normally do this with women you've only known for a few hours?'

Thomas shrugged. 'Depends if I like them or not.'

'Oh.' I took that to mean he liked me.

'We don't have to do anything. We can just hold hands if you want.'

'I think I can manage that,' I replied. My heart started beating faster as Thomas's warm palm slid into mine.

'I may have jumped the gun, sorry. I thought you would've cottoned on when I suggested lying down,' he said.

'I didn't, but s'ok.'

Since he'd apologised and didn't seem to expect anything other than hand holding, I calmed down.

'There. Isn't this lovely?' he said deadpan, and the ridiculousness of the situation made me want to giggle again. 'But I have enjoyed hanging out with you tonight,' he added.

Something in Thomas's voice made me turn my head on the pillow, and I saw he was looking at me in that way again, like he wanted to kiss me. Feeling nervous but also tempted, I swivelled my head back. I couldn't kiss Thomas, could I? Not when I was so enamoured with Jeremy. It would be tantamount to leading him on. But I did like him. Maybe it was best to be honest.

I cleared my throat. 'Since we're forging a path of clear communication, there are two things you should know about me.'

There was a pause. 'Er, OK. What are they?' asked Thomas warily.

'Ever since my long-term boyfriend cheated on me with my twin sister, I haven't been with a man. I think I might have a sexual phobia.'

'Riiight.'

'And ...' I paused to summon courage. 'I'm wretchedly in love with someone.'

Thomas didn't say anything for a minute, then propped

himself up on his elbow and peered down at me. The covers fell away from his chest, and I tried not to ogle, but his pecs were well defined; there was also a suggestion of abs going on. I felt a little worried that he was going to kick me out of his flat after my admission. But what he said next suggested he wasn't upset, just intrigued.

'So how is that going to work?'

'What do you mean?'

'Well, what if you find out this guy likes you too and wants to have sex? I assume it is a guy.'

I nodded. 'It's a guy. And I suppose the sex part would be an obstacle. But he doesn't like me, so it's a moot point.'

Thomas grunted. 'Dunno why he wouldn't want to go there. You've got me naked and raring to go. Maybe you should tell him how you feel. You never know.'

I was pleased Thomas had found me attractive enough to shed his clothes. But telling Jeremy? I shuddered under the duvet. 'There's no way I'm *ever* going to do that.'

'Who's the lucky fellow then? Someone at work?'

I pursed my lips, blushed hotly, and didn't reply.

Thomas grunted. 'Yeah, I thought so. Jeremy Trelawny. You were gushing about him in the pub.'

I cringed. Dammit. I really had to stop doing that dreamy voice thing!

'So you're lusting after him, and he's oblivious.'

I closed my eyes, feeling the usual wave of despair wash over me. 'Pretty much. When I don't see him, I'm in anguish. But then he rings and wants a meeting, so I'm in seventh heaven. The build-up is nerve-wracking: Seeing him is like a dream. Then it's over, and I want to fling myself off the faculty roof because I have to wait for him to ring and set up the next meeting. It's a hellish emotional roller coaster.'

'Sounds like a Shakespearean tragedy to me. But I can see why you wouldn't want to say anything.'

'Definitely.' I nodded, glad that Thomas understood where I was coming from.

'Yeah. Because if he found out how you felt and there was a chance he felt the same way, then you'd have the sex phobia issue.'

Oh. OK, he didn't quite understand where I was coming from. However, his different take on the situation got me thinking. There had been no doubt in my mind that my love for Jeremy was unrequited. But what if I was wrong? What if Jeremy was into me and as afraid as I was to show how he felt because we worked together? I hadn't considered that. He *did* insist on making me espresso and buying me salad. Had I been missing the signals he was sending? Hope rose in me like a miraculously blooming dead flower.

'If he did feel the same way, I'm sure I'd be able to deal

with ... getting intimate. We'd take it slow,' I told Thomas confidently. However, Jeremy was very sexually experienced. What if he found me woefully inadequate in bed and was put off from the get-go?

As if reading my mind, Thomas gave a doubtful 'hmmm' like he wasn't at all sure I would be able to deal with it.

'Well, if you need help—with the sex part, not the love part—I'm willing to offer my services,' he said.

'What?'

'Just saying, I'm pretty good at sex. So I could help you get back on the horse.'

I laughed in disbelief, though my madge did give quite a traitorous twang at the thought of having sex with Thomas. As Shakespeare wrote, 'Frailty, thy name is woman.' But then again, I *was* in bed with a naked good-looking guy!

'I'm sure I'll be fine,' I said primly. 'But thanks anyway.'

'No problem.'

Thomas shifted onto his back and laced his hands behind his head. We lay there in companionable silence, staring at the ceiling, his lava lamp casting a reddish-purple glow while its globs of colour morphed.

'So why do you think you're so good at sex anyway?' I asked eventually out of curiosity. 'Is that because someone told you, or you have a high opinion of yourself?'

'You can usually tell if someone is having a good time.'

'But what if they're faking it?'

'Nah, I've got the moves.'

'Like what?'

Thomas jutted his hips backwards and forward and did a circular thrusting motion underneath the cover. 'Something like that. Gets them going.'

I snorted. 'How romantic.'

'We could try it if you like.'

I swallowed. 'Maybe not.'

'We don't have to have penetrative sex anyway. There are always other things we can do if you need some practise.'

'Like?'

'Kissing, earlobe sucking, nipple tweaking, genital stimulation ...' Thomas counted them off on his fingers.

'OK, OK, I get the idea,' I said hastily.

'I've got a toy you might like actually.'

I shook my head. 'No, I don't think so.'

'How do you know if you've never tried it?'

'I just know I wouldn't,' I stated.

Maybe it was my narrow-minded attitude or he really wanted me to try his toy, but Thomas flipped open the bedside drawer and brought out a large pink penis-shaped vibrator.

'Oh my god! That's huge!'

He grinned. 'It's comparable.'

'Why on earth do you have that *thing* in your drawer?'

'A girl I was seeing left it behind. I found it in the bathroom cupboard a few weeks after we'd broken up. It didn't end well, so I felt justified in keeping it.'

'Maybe your moves weren't satisfying her.'

'No, but her yoga instructor's were.'

I winced. 'Oh, sorry.'

Thomas flipped the switch on the thing, and it started juddering. He stuck it under the bedcover and touched my leg with it, and I let out a yelp at the weird sensation.

'Relax, it won't hurt you. Look, I'll run it up and down your thigh so you get used to it.'

'Is it clean?'

'Of course. Now close your eyes and pretend it's Jeremy's.'

I let out a sigh, thinking of the lovely clay penis I'd flattened last night. 'Well, OK. But keep it on my thigh,' I cautioned.

Really, this impromptu date was getting stranger by the minute.

Chapter 10

I didn't see Jasper for the rest of the day or the day after that, so I was able to regain some sense of myself. The dream had shaken me badly but it was just a dream after all. If I ever, by some miracle, found myself in his bed I couldn't imagine not wanting him, so I thrust it from my thoughts.

On the third afternoon, I was sitting with Sebastian in the library room while he explained the meaning of one of Shakespeare's sonnets to me. I wasn't sure what Mother would think of me learning Shakespeare, but I considered that Mother didn't need to know.

The day of my nineteenth birthday had come and gone some weeks ago, and she had sent me a present of a hooded cloak. It was neither fashionable nor new, but it was warm, and for that, I was grateful. I had not seen either her or my sister since I had left, and Mother had not invited me home to visit. Father's death lay heavy and painful between us, and I didn't know how to resolve it.

Sebastian's petulant sigh broke through my musings. 'It's no use. I've been prattling on for the last fifteen minutes, and you haven't listened to a word I've said. It's all very well to expound on the merits of the iambic pentameter, but I'm starting to bore myself!'

'Sorry, sir,' I said, feeling bad for not attending. 'I'm not quite myself today. Could we come back to it another time?'

'Yes, we'll have to. Besides, I've got a Bible studies class in here shortly. It's too cold outside ...' We both turned to look at the icy garden with its bare-boughed trees. 'Just a couple of the local lads, uh-hum. I thought we'd take a look at Revelations and then have toast and tea—' He stopped abruptly as if realising he was rambling.

I got up to leave, and Sebastian tidied his papers. 'Oh, I almost forgot! Jasper asked me to give this to you this morning before he went out.' My heart stopped and then started thudding painfully in my chest.

'W-what is it?' I asked, trying to breathe normally. Sebastian handed me a letter with my name scrawled on the front in swirly black ink.

'I don't know. I tried to look inside, but I wasn't too successful. It's sealed firmly with his family crest.'

I turned the letter over and blinked. Sure enough, there was a red wax seal.

'It's some foolishness, I'm sure. Don't take it too seriously—Jasper likes a joke except when it's on him, of course.'

I nodded, took the envelope, and went upstairs as quickly as I could. Here it was, my summons. I was sure I wasn't going to like it, whatever it was. I sat on the bed and looked at the letter. It sat there innocently in my palm— small, white, and square. The red wax seal had the impression of a lion and a sword. I gulped, impressed despite myself. Jasper's heritage was undeniable; he came from old money, and he wasn't afraid to show it.

Gingerly, I broke the seal and opened the flaps. Inside, there was the same swirly black writing. I managed to read it by sounding out the words. It said that Mr Jasper Donne, Esq. was desirous of my company two nights hence for supper in the dining room at eight o'clock sharp. No RSVP required. That was it. I sat there deliberating. An invite to dine with him? Just me? What about Sebastian and Maggie—whatever would they think?

Then as I suppose he knew it would, my disbelief turned into pleasure. Whatever it meant and as suspicious as I was, an invitation to spend the whole evening with Jasper was not to be turned down lightly. In fact, I hadn't even considered turning it down. In hindsight, perhaps it would have been a better idea.

Two days in some minds might not be a long time. In my mind, it was an eternity. I continuously rode one wave of sheer terror and then another of sheer ecstasy and experienced a sea of every emotion in between.

In my saner moments, I had practical concerns. What should I wear to this supper? I couldn't show up in my maid's dress—it was just too drab for words. Fortunately, my wages were plentiful enough that, after sending a portion to my mother each week, I had been saving the rest in a leather money purse. This meant I could afford to buy something to wear in town.

On the morning of the supper rendezvous, I asked Maggie if I could visit the butcher's for her since she always had a roast of some sort planned for Saturday. To my surprise, Maggie said that she was spending the evening at her sister's, so she wouldn't be cooking, but I could pick up some flowers at the market if I liked. Apparently, Mr Donne had specifically requested fresh flowers for this evening.

My heart leapt. These two things in themselves—Maggie out for the evening and flowers requested by Jasper—meant that it certainly seemed as if the evening were to take place. I had had my doubts, but it looked as if he was managing to engineer it.

Cautiously, I enquired about Sebastian. 'And Father Fannon, will he be requiring supper this eve?'

'Ah, no,' said Maggie, deftly gutting a fresh fish as she spoke. 'Father is visiting the next village for a Bible session with some of the local lads and then staying overnight with a friend. He'll be back tomorrow morn. So it'll just be you and Mr Donne tonight.'

There was a silence. She looked at me, and I felt my face go redder than it normally was.

'Don't mind 'im. He's easy enough to please. Give 'im some bread and some of this fish.' She picked up a large knife and brought it down on the fish in one loud banging stroke, effectively cutting off its head. 'That should do 'im quite well.' Queasily, I backed out of the kitchen.

It was bitterly cold when I stepped outside with my basket. Shivering, I drew up the hood of my cloak and set off towards town. As I walked with my coins jingling in my pocket, I thought about the impossibility of the house's main occupants, Maggie and Sebastian, both being out on this very night. It had to be Jasper; he had to have organised it somehow, and this knowledge eased some of my doubts.

At the town market, some late flowering sweet peas were on sale, so I bought a bunch of white ones for my basket. I considered red roses but didn't want to be too presumptuous. The dress was harder to source. But I went to the rag fair, which was held every Saturday morning in the narrow street next to the parish church. On a table of old clothing, I found an evening skirt made of dark-blue wool with the hem coming down. But I could fix that up without any trouble. I was still no beauty, but it should fit me well and look seemly with my white blouse and green bodice.

Back at the house, the rest of the day passed in a dream. I had seen neither hide nor hair of Jasper all day, so I had no idea what he was doing about supper. I hoped we wouldn't be eating fish on toast. Perhaps he was transporting it here on silver platters in horse-drawn carriages. That was too unbelievable, even for my vivid imagination.

As it turned half past six o'clock, then seven o'clock and Maggie and Sebastian had both left somewhere in between, my stomach started churning with nerves. I paced the room, wringing my hands in despair. The thought of sitting across a table from Jasper, making polite conversation, was incredible. Was it really going to happen? I felt like I might faint from expectation.

At a quarter to eight, I put on my new-old blue skirt with its carefully repaired hem, a clean white blouse, and laced up my green bodice. I sat on the bed feeling a bit foolish.

Who did I think I was? I was a lowly housemaid—not good enough to have supper with someone of Jasper's breeding and status. I almost started crying from the confusion and stress of it all. But then I remembered my father and how he used to look at me with such pride in his eyes and tell me what a good girl I was and how much he loved me. I squared my shoulders and tied my hair back with his ribbon. I might only be a blacksmith's daughter, but I had survived the pox, and I had the scars to prove it.

It was eight o'clock. I crept out of my room and down the stairs. The house was dark and very quiet. I made my way to the dining room. A soft light flickered from underneath the door. I imagined many lit candles would make such a light. The fragrance of orange and honey from the sweet peas drifted to my nose. In my mind's eye, I saw the white flowers as the centrepiece of the table, which was laid with the good linen cloth and set for two with polished silverware.

Hardly daring to breathe, I opened the door and went in. Incredibly, it was as I'd imagined. Candles had been lit and placed around the room, giving off a soft yellow glow; and in the centre of the room, a table was set for two with the good linen and silver cutlery. The flowers I was mistaken about. The sweet peas were on the sideboard. In the centre of the table was a glass vase holding a single red rose.

There was no sign of Jasper. I went to the table and sat down. I listened. Nothing but the hiss and spit of the candles and the trees rustling outside in the wind. After a good ten minutes went past, I became restless. Where was he? Then I heard carriage wheels coming up the drive.

I smoothed my skirt with trembling hands, waiting. But strangely I heard a woman's voice outside. Had he brought a serving maid with him? Footsteps came to the front door and entered the hallway. I heard a woman's high-pitched giggle and a man say something. It was Jasper.

At that moment, I had a strong sense that I shouldn't be here. I went hot, then cold. This was bad, very bad. But I had no time to do anything.

The door opened; and in swept Jasper, resplendent in a black frock coat under which he wore a magenta waistcoat and black breeches. Following directly behind him was a young woman dressed in a tightly corseted gold silk gown with frothy white sleeves. Her beauty took my breath away. She had shining blonde hair swept up in some complicated hairstyle I could never in my life hope to imitate and a flawless ivory complexion. Diamonds glinted in her ears and glimmered from the jewel-encrusted necklace at her swanlike throat.

'Ah, Mercy,' said Jasper, smiling at me guilelessly. 'This is Lady Arabella de La Croix. Arabella, this is Mercy, our maid who will be serving us this evening.'

My heart plummeted to my toes at his words, but I took care not to move a muscle. Arabella looked at me with piercing blue eyes; she didn't say hello. I saw her note every pockmark on my face, and her small nose wrinkled with disapproval.

'Then why, pray tell,' she said, looking at Jasper pointedly, 'is she sitting at our table?'

Jasper's eyes glinted mischievously. 'I don't know,' he

said. 'Perhaps she decided to keep the seat warm for you. She's good for things like that. Mercy, we'd like our entrée now please. Arabella my dear, why don't you be seated?'

I got up slowly and watched Arabella flounce over, settle herself in my seat, and arrange her mass of golden skirts. I was so shocked by the turn of events I couldn't say a word. I just stood there and kept staring at Jasper, who must've felt the weight of my gaze but didn't flinch once. He got some Madeira out of the sideboard and poured two glasses. When he sat down, he looked at me.

'What, Mercy? Am I not paying you enough for this little extra service? I think you'll find I am when you go into the kitchen.' Arabella whispered something, and he chuckled. 'No, she's not simple. She's actually becoming very well educated. Sebastian's making sure of that. I'll tell you about it over our entrée, when it finally arrives. By the way, Mercy, can you take these flowers away? They're giving me a headache.'

I curtsied abruptly and sidled out of the room clutching the vase of sweet peas leaving the two of them alone—Arabella sipping her Madeira and Jasper gazing at her adoringly.

Chapter 11

Thomas insisted on walking me home. After saying goodbye, I headed straight for the shower, turned the dial to hot, and stood underneath, so the steaming water would scald away the memories of what we'd done.

Eleanor's comment about me needing to feel the sting of pleasure with someone was coming back to haunt me. I groaned. If I'd known her good-looking cousin was a master vibrator wielder, I wouldn't have let him anywhere near me with that thing. But it was too late now. What was done was done.

To his credit, Thomas had kept up a steady stream of commentary, asking if what he was doing was OK. I supposed he was worried because I'd said I had a sexual phobia and didn't want me to freak out. I don't know why I'd said that, but after Ben left me, I felt anxious about going on dates and it leading to sex. So I'd assumed I had now had one.

I had appreciated Thomas's concern, but part of me wished he would be quiet and let me fantasise about Jeremy. However, when he'd absently shifted the thing into the apex of my thighs, I discovered that having a large vibrator between my legs was immensely pleasurable. I'd let out a strangled gasp.

'Whoops, sorry about that,' Thomas apologised, hastily moving it away.

'No, it's fine. You can keep it there,' I said, trying not to sound overly eager.

'Well, if you insist.' He moved it back and began making small stroking movements, centring it on a certain spot. My eyelids fluttered closed as I felt a pleasurable warmth travel up from between my legs and swirl around my solar plexus. A small moan escaped before I could help it.

Recognising I was feeling amorous, Thomas said, 'Shall I kiss you? It might make it feel less clinical ...'

'OK,' I agreed, more conducive to the idea of snogging him.

Thomas lowered his lips to mine, and we kissed while he continued stroking me with the vibrator. He was a good kisser, not sloppy and didn't try to ram his tongue down my throat, which I appreciated. Kissing him was actually pretty great, and he was obviously enjoying it too from the small noises he was making in his throat. As the kissing and vibrating went on with no traumatic effects (only enjoyable ones), I found myself automatically stroking his bare chest.

My hand dropped lower, feeling his washboard abs, and lower until I accidentally touched his member, which was warm and stiff. Embarrassed, I drew my hand away, but he said, 'Feel free to go there.'

Then he added, 'Or not. I don't mind.'

'Maybe I should take off my clothes too,' I said, avoiding his eyes.

He shrugged. 'Sure. Just tell me if at any point you want me to stop.'

I soaped my body thoroughly twice, rinsed, turned the water off, and reached for a towel. I buried my face in it and let out another groan as visions of Thomas steadily going through his checklist invaded my brain. At no point had I told him to stop. That was because everything he'd done had felt really good. Placing the vibrator so it buzzed away between my legs, he'd nibbled my earlobe, then sucked my nipples; and it was fantastic. And I'd participated by stroking his length, which he assured me felt equally as good. It was all so good, in fact, that things progressed to the point that we'd spontaneously climaxed. Afterwards, as we lay there, coming to our senses, Thomas had quipped, 'Well, that was fun.'

At the time, it *had* been fun and strangely freeing since there was no pressure or expectations involved, but now I wondered what the hell I'd done. I felt guilty, like I'd somehow betrayed Jeremy, which was ridiculous. He was probably off having his own orgasms and not giving me a second thought. Or was he?

It was well after midnight when I'd finished drying my hair and was settled in bed, wearing a clean camisole and knickers. Idly, I glanced at my phone on the nightstand and saw there was a message from 'Thomas the Tank Engine'. My heart sank, then, confusingly, lifted.

After Thomas had walked me home, there was the inevitable discussion about exchanging numbers. He'd wanted to put his in my contacts, but I hadn't wanted him to see what I'd named him. So to get out of that dilemma, I'd confessed I already had his number and messaged him so he had mine. Now he'd sent me one back.

TTTE: *Hi, I had a great time tonight. I know I said that before we did stuff, but just to reiterate it. Hope you're not freaking out because of your sex phobia. Let me know you're OK.*

I supposed if I didn't reply, he'd think I was freaking out. He did sound like he genuinely cared about my well-being. Either that, or he was worried I'd tell Eleanor that he'd seduced me.

Me: *Hi, no, I'm not freaking out. Well, a little. But it had been a while, so to be expected I guess.*

TTTE: *I didn't ask about what happened because I didn't want to pry but for the record what your boyfriend and sister did to you was pretty shit.*

Me: *Yes it was. But perhaps tonight was exactly what I needed to get back on the horse as you said.*

TTTE: *Any chance you'll need more practise?*

Me: *Let me sleep on it and I'll get back to you.*

***

A man who wanted me for my body rather than my heart was better than no man at all, I reasoned. Besides, I needed to be on top form sexually to entice Jeremy. I had to have *moves*, and Thomas was willing to teach me his. There didn't seem to be any catch that I could see; emotions weren't involved. He was simply in it to have some fun and to 'help a girl out'. Once that fun was over and the girl was brought up to speed, I assumed he'd move on to someone else. Of course, it went without saying that Eleanor wouldn't be privy to this arrangement. He said as much when I called him the next morning, and we arranged for him to drop by my flat in the late afternoon.

'Er, you're not going to mention this to Eleanor, are you? I'd prefer it if she didn't know.'

'I wasn't planning on it. She said she didn't want details if I met up with you anyway.'

'Good.'

So our rendezvous took on a clandestine air. It was quite exciting. I'd never been anyone's naughty little secret before. I tended to be the one finding out about other people's naughty little secrets.

Even though it was Sunday, being the owner of an e-bike shop meant that Thomas said he often needed to work weekends to give his staff time off. However, he could take his pick of bikes. When I opened the door to his buzz just after 4 p.m., he was in a tight black muscle T-shirt and khaki cargo shorts, propping up a shiny red bike.

'Do you mind if I bring it inside? It's brand new. If I chained it up, it would probably get nicked in five seconds.'

'Of course.' I stepped aside as he wheeled it into the hallway.

As he passed by, I caught the pleasing scent of spicy deodorant and light sweat, and my stomach flipped nervously. He had the kind of larger-than-life presence that tended to command attention. I couldn't help checking him out as he propped the bike against the wall, appreciating his athletic body. He turned and saw me watching him.

'Hey.' Thomas came over and kissed me on the lips without any preamble. His confidence was reassuring. He wasn't going to play hard to get. He knew what he was here for and what would be happening.

Checking out my white jeans and blue cotton shirt, he said, 'You look nice. No disguise today?'

'No, that didn't work. The guy I was stalking saw right through it.'

Thomas grinned and ran his hand through his hair. 'Can I grab some water before we … ?'

'Sure,' I said, leading the way to the kitchen.

I filled a glass with water at the sink, and he leaned against the counter next to me, sipping it and stroking my arm. I shivered involuntarily at his touch. 'So no ill effects after last night? No rocking in the corner, night terrors, or anything?'

I shook my head. 'I slept like a log.'

'Good. I knew I'd cure you.'

I laughed. 'Maybe you have. Maybe you haven't.'

He finished his water, put the glass down, and moved closer so he was pressing me up against the counter. 'No?'

My heart beat faster seeing his face at close range. His cheeks were flushed, his eyes half lidded. 'You smell nice,' he said. 'Like strawberries.'

'You do too, like a pine forest.'

Thomas chuckled. 'You really have a way with words.'

He leaned in and kissed me, his tongue slowly caressing mine. I felt the stir of desire between my legs for the second time in less than twenty-four hours.

When we broke apart, he said, 'I've been thinking about you all day. There I was, amongst the bike parts when I wanted to be amongst your parts.'

I giggled at that.

He lifted me onto the counter, and caught up in the moment, I hooked my legs around his waist. But then I realised that we were making out in my kitchen, where I cooked my meals.

'What am I doing?' I said aloud as Thomas proceeded to unbutton my shirt. He pulled the cup of my bra down to gently suck on an exposed nipple.

'I don't know,' he murmured. 'But I don't think you should stop.'

***

Thomas seemed content to continue in the kitchen, but I suggested we move things to my bedroom. Since I'd changed the sheets, vacuumed, and dusted every single inch of it (even the top of the wardrobe and skirting boards) while waiting for him to come over, it seemed a waste not to.

Not that he cared about dusty architraves. The only cobwebs he seemed interested in clearing away were mine.

After a similar interaction to last night's (except that Thomas nimbly used his fingers instead of a vibrator), again, I willingly succumbed to his expert touch. I was surprised that I felt so comfortable with him, or maybe it was because I knew I couldn't get hurt. My heart belonged to someone else. Even if he could manipulate my body in pleasurable ways, love was always going to be off-limits.

After pulling on his boxer briefs and using the bathroom, Thomas walked around my bedroom, looking at things, while I lay in bed with the sheet pulled over me. I watched him trace the titles on the bookshelf, finger the midnight-blue silk runner with silver stars covering the dresser, and pick up my cat ornament and peer closely at it. I twitched a little, not used to having someone inspect my personal stuff. Eventually, he sat on the side of the bed. I wondered if I should provide tea, coffee, or juice now the deed was done.

'Do you live alone?' he asked.

'Yes.'

'How come?'

'I prefer it. Do you?' I hadn't thought to ask him before.

'No, I have a flatmate.'

'Oh. Guy or girl?'

'Guy. I don't see him much. He usually stays at his

girlfriend's place.'

'Ah.'

He looked at me and chewed his bottom lip. 'Should I go? I mean, I don't want to. But if I'm in the way ...'

I hitched the sheet higher. 'You don't have to go. We can chat as well as ... the other, surely.'

'True. Fancy a cuppa? I'll make it.'

'OK, yes, thanks.'

'How do you have it? Let me guess—white, no sugar.'

'Actually, white with half a sugar.'

He snapped his fingers. 'I'll have to remember that.'

I wondered how many cups of tea he was planning on making for me during our short acquaintance.

Lying there listening to the sound of him humming in the kitchen as he sorted the tea was quite soothing. I thought I should probably get dressed or at least put my knickers on, but I couldn't be bothered. My limbs and other bits felt lovely and relaxed after his attention.

Thomas brought in two mugs of steaming tea and went to place mine on top of Mercy's memoir, which was on my bedside table.

'Don't put it on there!' I screeched, flinging out an arm to stop him.

'Wow, OK.' Thomas stood there holding the tea, looking startled.

I snatched the green book up from the table and held it to my chest. 'Sorry, it's just really old, from an archive. A hot mug of tea on the binding would be extremely damaging. You need to put on white gloves to even read it.'

Thomas's eyes narrowed. 'If it's so old, why have you got it here in the first place? Shouldn't it be at your office?'

'I'm kind of doing a private reading. It's OK. I'm being careful with it.' I opened my bedside drawer, pulled on a pair of white gloves, and put on my owl-rimmed glasses.

Thomas groaned.

'What?'

'You look like a hot librarian.'

I rolled my eyes. 'Whatever. Now listen, this is what's happened to Mercy so far. It's fascinating.'

I filled Thomas in on the backstory while he sat on the bed next to me with his legs crossed at the ankles, sipping tea.

'So what's this guy Jasper's deal?'

'I don't know. But now he's invited her to dinner, and she got all excited about it, but it's a mean trick. He's turned up with this awful woman, Arabella, instead ...'

Chapter 12

Upon leaving the dining room, I ran into two smartly dressed footmen in dark-blue velvet suits with gold buttons who had been busily transferring silver cloches to the kitchen table.

'Supper for the lady and master,' said one, bowing swiftly in my direction, and then they took their leave. I heard the faint crunching of carriage wheels on the gravel outside.

As soon as I entered the kitchen and saw all the gleaming silver cloches, my heart sank. My imagination hadn't been too vivid after all. Jasper had outdone himself by enlisting the help of some upper-class cook. Unfortunately, it wasn't with me in mind. Tentatively, I lifted the cloche of the nearest dish, which contained some kind of broth. It smelt rich and delicious. But my own appetite had disappeared entirely. I considered not going through with it, but I knew I had to; it was my duty as a maid.

From the dining room came gales of mirth from Arabella. Perhaps Jasper was telling her the amusing tale of my education or enlightening her about my humble background, where the likes of me weren't able to escape the horrors of smallpox because we had no country house to hole up in. We just had to endure it and put up with people's condemnation afterwards and then work as servants for the rest of our lives.

I looked at my face, which was reflected in one of the silver cloches. And then I looked again. A cruel trick of the light had blocked out the worst of the scars so the face looking back at me was smooth and unmarked. I appeared almost normal. This was how I was meant to look—not the scarred freak the pox had made me.

My confidence rose. Perhaps I could get through this if I kept that image of myself in my head. I grabbed the dish containing the soup and carried it into the dining room.

'Ah, Mercy, finally!' said Jasper, rising and taking the dish from me. 'We thought you'd decided to eat the entrée yourself.'

Arabella snickered.

'Of course not,' I said. 'I was organising things in the kitchen. Would you like some more wine?'

I grabbed the bottle and sloshed it into their glasses, managing to spill a few drops on Arabella's smooth bouncing bosom.

'Watch it, servant!' she snarled and dabbed delicately at her cleavage. Jasper looked amused.

'Now, now, darling, be nice,' he soothed. 'Let me feed you some soup. That should cheer you up.'

He scooped up a spoonful and fed it into Arabella's waiting open mouth. I could hardly bear to watch as her tongue flicked out like a snake and licked the spoon clean.

Jasper's chocolate-brown eyes found mine. 'Still here? You really are a sucker for punishment,' they seemed to say.

I left the room in a nauseous daze. In the kitchen, I held on to the counter for dear life. The sight of Jasper feeding Arabella had almost made me come undone. Misery welled in me, and I felt like bursting into tears.

Then I spied, tucked beneath one of the serving dishes, a letter sealed with red wax and my name on it. Gingerly, I broke the seal, and a few coins slid out. I gathered this was the payment for the 'extra service' Jasper had mentioned. I felt sick again and tossed the coins back on the table. I had obviously read the invitation wrong. Or I had read it correctly, and he'd decided to play a cruel trick, knowing how I felt about him—that I was the fool was in no doubt.

'Jasper likes a joke except when it's on him,' Sebastian had said. Could I somehow turn this joke around so it was no longer on me? What ammunition did I possibly have? Then I remembered. Jasper's letter—the one I'd found in his wardrobe and never opened out of some false sense of propriety, hoping for a chance to put it back undiscovered.

Well, the gloves were off now. If I had to go into that room one more time and witness him flirting with Arabella ... I shuddered. I calculated I had about ten minutes before they started clamouring for their first course. I ran up the kitchen stairs, along the hallway, and up into my room, looking around wildly. Where had I put it? The dresser. I pulled out all the drawers and flung my underthings into the air. It had to be here. Yes! In the bottom drawer.

I stood there holding the envelope for what seemed like an age. I had never knowingly opened another person's private mail for the purpose of revenge. Yet for all its wrongness, it felt right in this case. Taking a deep breath, I opened the flaps and unfolded the sheet of paper. Thumbmarks were all over it, and the paper was old and very creased, as if it had been read a thousand times. I inferred from this that the letter was very important to Jasper. I eagerly scanned its contents, thanking the lord and Sebastian that I could read.

After I finished the letter, I stood there like a statue for some minutes, struggling to absorb it. I couldn't quite believe the irony of life. Either that, or God had revealed himself to me in the lines of a quivering cursive script. I felt a glimmer of hope. If this were to be the longest night of my life, then by some quirk of fate, I had acquired the internal armour with which to bear the blows.

Throwing back my shoulders, I steeled myself and headed back down to the kitchen to serve the lovers their first course. Upon lifting several of the cloches, I discovered roast quail, which was rapidly losing heat. Still, the aroma emanating from the silver dish was so delicious my appetite returned, and it was all I could do to stop myself from ripping one of the tiny thighs to shreds with my teeth. My anger was reaching boiling point as I stormed through to the dining room.

Unfortunately, I didn't have time to rearrange my features, and some of what I was feeling must have shown on my face. Eagle-eyed Jasper missed nothing.

'Everything all right, Mercy? I was beginning to get a bit worried—worried we might not get our next course, that is.'

Arabella smirked and smoothed her golden hair. I felt like tearing it out by the roots. Instead, I gritted my teeth and took the platter to the sideboard. I served the quail onto plates and brought them to the table. Arabella glanced at it.

'I can't eat this,' she said sharply.

Jasper looked pained. 'Why ever not, darling? It's fresh from your uncle's grounds this morning.'

'I'm sure it is. But have you forgotten I'm afraid of chickens?'

I couldn't help interjecting, 'It *is* dead, miss, I assure you.'

She swivelled around in her chair to fix me with her cold blue eyes. 'Did I ask for your opinion, maid? Hold your tongue!'

I swear my mouth moved on its own accord, or perhaps what I had read in the letter made me bold.

'But how can you be afraid if it's the size of a mouse and not moving?' I asked. 'Besides, it's not chicken. It's quail. Even I know that.'

Arabella's mouth dropped open at my insolence. Jasper looked at me, and I stared back unflinchingly. He saw that I was unafraid of him but didn't know why.

'Are you going to sit there and let her talk to me like that?' complained Arabella. There was a terse silence from Jasper. 'Well?'

'If you don't want your quail, I'll have it,' Jasper said slowly. 'Perhaps Maggie will rustle you up an omelette. I think I heard her come in just now. Unless you're afraid of eggs as well?'

He looked at me, expressionless. 'That'll be all for tonight, Mercy. Maggie can serve us the rest of our supper.'

And with those words, a warm glow settled somewhere in the region of my chest. I was off the hook, and even better, he'd stood up for me. I floated off upstairs, leaving Maggie to deal with Arabella's dietary complaints. I had gained some power through what I had read in the letter, and I held that knowledge close to me like a protective cloak. He must never know that I knew.

In my room, I disrobed and put on my nightdress. I felt unbearably tired, not to mention hungry. I shut my eyes and prepared to go to sleep. A few minutes later, noises in the hallway downstairs disturbed me—footsteps, a giggle being shushed. Then all was quiet, and I shut my eyes again.

But shortly afterwards, a soft thump reverberated up the wall; and I sat up, startled. Then there was another thump and another. And then a woman moaned softly, the sound floating up through the floorboards. A cold hand gripped my heart and slowly squeezed it until I couldn't breathe. Jasper's room was directly below mine, but surely, he wouldn't do that? He'd stood up for me against her; he'd shown he respected me. Arabella was now making high-pitched cries of pleasure as Jasper thumped her up against the wall. This couldn't be happening. Surely, he must know the pain this would cause me?

Arabella's groans reached a crescendo; obviously, she didn't care who heard her. A black cloud of depression overwhelmed me, and I curled up into a tight ball with my hands over my ears to try to block out the noise. My only comfort was the knowledge that I now had. I knew why Jasper's hand had shaken so badly upon first seeing me. The pox was his nemesis.

3rd May 1760
Brockenhill Manor
Oxfordshire

Dear Jasper,

This letter will come as a shock to you no doubt. And I pity myself for being the one to tell you, but tell you I must. Your poor dear mother, father, sister and brother perished from the pox two weeks past.

I did not send a message to your school before now because I have just received the terrible news myself. The family friend who wrote to me said they did not suffer, as those from the illness have been known to do. The passing was quick, as was their burial. Your father's will has specified that I am to be your guardian and you are, of course, most welcome here after your term ends.

Your loving and grieving uncle,
Jonathan Donne

Chapter 13

Thomas stayed for dinner. The descriptions of Jasper and Arabella's supper had made both of us hungry. I couldn't offer him roast quail but rustled up tomato soup and grilled cheese on toast instead.

'The letter still doesn't explain Jasper's behaviour,' said Thomas, dunking a piece of cheesy toast into his soup. We were sitting at the kitchen table, having a discussion about the memoir. 'OK, he hates the pox because of what it did to his family. But why is he playing a game of cat and mouse with Mercy? Why bother?'

I slurped a spoonful of soup. 'Because he's an alpha male who likes to feel powerful and gets off on seeing her squirm. Back then, men ruled the roost. You know that. Women were seen as breeding machines or tossed aside once they'd been sullied.'

'So he plans to sully her?'

I shook my head. 'I don't think so, but she definitely needs to watch out. He's a real piece of work.'

'You'll have to keep reading and let me know how it goes with Jasper.' He paused. 'And with Jeremy.'

I ducked my head and concentrated on my soup.

Thomas left soon after saying he had an early start in the

morning. That was fine with me. I didn't particularly like the idea of sharing my bed with him. But if he'd wanted to stay, I would've said yes. But I slept like the proverbial log without giving it too much thought.

The next morning, I was rifling through my wardrobe, looking for something to wear to work. But nothing seemed right. I yanked boring top after boring top along on their hangers until I came to the designer work dress that I'd bought in a moment of confidence a while back. When I'd modelled it for Eleanor and Lily one evening, their mouths had formed twin O shapes.

'Anna, you can't wear that to work,' Eleanor had said, sounding shocked.

'Why not? It was in the business wear section of the shop.' It was a black bodycon number that ended at midthigh, with a keyhole neck. Honestly, it looked more a dress you'd wear to a nightclub. But I liked it.

'Because it's inappropriate,' replied Eleanor.

'Oh, don't be so stuffy, Nor. It looks amazing on her. And there isn't a dress code, is there?' Lily argued, ever the defender of inappropriate clothing.

Eleanor had cocked an eyebrow, looking me over. 'No, but what kind of "business" would she be conducting in that?'

Her comment had put me right off, thinking the dress was too slutty and I'd poked it into the back of my wardrobe, thinking I'd save it for a date evening, then never went on a date.

I held the dress up and looked at it, wondering if I dared. My mind flashed back to yesterday afternoon in bed with Thomas—his deep brown eyes boring into mine as he touched me, murmuring how sexy I was, how much I turned him on. My confidence rose. If I wanted Jeremy to see me as something more than a boring research assistant, I had to change it up.

Fuck it, I thought. *Why not? Let's get slutty.*

I wore my knee-length beige trench over the dress, effectively concealing it, but my black heels and glossy tan back-seamed stockings were very much on show. By the time I reached the faculty, I'd garnered at least half a dozen double takes. My confidence grew further. I was turning men's heads! A nervous excitement fluttered in my gut as I wondered what kind of reaction I'd get from Jeremy. I'd never flaunted myself so brazenly before, and the thought that I might actually snag his attention made me giddy.

Another image of Thomas materialised: the soft smile he'd given me as he'd leaned in and given me a swift kiss on the cheek before he left. I quickly pushed it aside.

This wasn't about him. He knew my deal from the start. I doubted very much if he was even thinking about me.

Of course, wearing a sexy dress to work to titillate Jeremy was one thing. Actually, having him see me in it was another. We had no meeting scheduled for today. Becca had the morning off visiting the dentist, thankfully. So I was alone in our office. I glared at the Jeremy hotline, willing it to ring. *Come on!* Was I going to have to spend ages on my hair and make-up and wear this dress every day for the whole week?

I was indulging in a pleasant day dream about Thomas and how nice our time together had been when the Jeremy hotline rang.

I swiped the receiver off the cradle. 'Hello?' I said breathlessly.

'Morning, Anna. Could you pop in for a quick word?'

Jeremy's sexy, self-assured tone sent endorphins speeding through my veins like crack cocaine.

'Of course. See you in five!' I exclaimed a little too loudly.

He hung up without replying.

I drew a large shaky breath and stood, my palms sweating. This was it. My summons. I checked for mascara smudges, reapplied my Cherry Blaze lipstick, and blotted, smacking my lips together on the folded piece of tissue like a crazed guppy.

Wobbling slightly in my heels, I made my way down the hallway, wishing there was a full-length mirror so I could check how I looked. Perhaps I should veer to the ladies'. But I'd said I'd be there in five minutes, and I didn't want to annoy him by being late—not when I wanted him to desire me.

I rapped, and Jeremy told me to come in. As per usual, he was absorbed in his laptop. He waved me over without looking up. I started on my short journey to the chair opposite, trying not to trip over the rug and the stacks of books lining my path like a runway. I wondered if he was this untidy at home. Just then, I noticed Jeremy had ceased reading, and his gaze was focused on my high heels. I froze like a burglar caught in a spotlight. His eyes travelled slowly up my stockings, traversed my torso, and kept inching higher until they lingered on my bust area and finally reached my face. My body felt seared, like he'd gone over me with a blowtorch. From his impassive expression, I couldn't tell what Jeremy was thinking. But one thing was certain: he'd definitely noticed the dress.

I sat down quickly with a nervous 'Morning. You wanted to see me?'

Jeremy seemed to shake himself out of some kind of

daze.

'Ah, yes. It's about the interviewees for Becca's job.' He leaned back in his chair and steepled his fingers. 'I've narrowed it down to Lucy Flanagan and Peter Wilson. The other girl didn't have strong-enough data analysis skills, and as you know, I have high standards.'

A starburst of pleasure erupted in my chest, knowing he included me in that 'high standard'. I said eagerly, 'I think Peter would be ideal. His referees both remarked on his attention to detail.'

Jeremy's eyes dropped to my Cherry Blaze lips and said thoughtfully, 'Hmm, I still think Lucy would be better. She ticks all the boxes.'

Grrrr. No!

'I don't agree,' I said pointedly, and Jeremy looked taken aback as I didn't normally challenge him.

'Why?' he asked.

I didn't have a good answer to that other than 'I've finally gotten you to notice me. There's no way in hell I want Irish Lucy stealing your attention'.

I opened my mouth and shut it again.

There was a short but tense silence as I battled to find a suitable reply that would suffice. During this time, Jeremy was displaying a rather pertinent interest in my dress, especially the keyhole bust area. I hadn't experienced this level of attention from him before. It was strange and somewhat unnerving. A slow flush of heat washed over my body. Jeremy's eyes flicked to mine, and I caught my breath, drowning in twin aqua cenote pools. Dear God. He truly was too beautiful to bear.

'I trust your d-decision. Well, I … I should get back. Lots of work to do,' I stuttered.

'Right. Yes, me too,' he said in a clipped professional tone.

Hastily, I got up and skedaddled towards the door. 'Good luck with the …' I said, turning and managing to catch him staring fixedly at my retreating bottom. 'Interviews,' I finished weakly.

Shutting the door behind me, I leaned against it, feeling slightly faint. Bloody hell. If I'd known Jeremy Trelawny was a sucker for a little black dress, I could've saved myself two years of anguish!

After the encounter in his office, I couldn't concentrate. I was meant to be cross-referencing some data, but all I could do was stare at my screen blankly, replaying how Jeremy had undressed me with his scorching eyes.

I felt his presence smouldering down the hall, like the end of a lit fuse slowly sparking its way towards a pile of dynamite. Was he really going to overstep the boundaries of our working relationship and ask me out? I could hardly believe it. But the heavy anticipation in the air lent a sharpening to my senses. Something was going to happen.

At half past four, there was a ping as an email dropped. When I saw it was from Jeremy, with the subject line 'Wednesday evening?', I almost had a heart attack. The fidget spinner I'd been playing with flew out of my hand and hit the opposite wall with a bang, just above Becca's head. 'Jesus!' she exclaimed. 'What's with you? You've been jumpy all afternoon.'

'Sorry,' I muttered.

I waited until Becca had left for the day and clicked on the email. My heart was thumping so hard I could feel it in my throat.

Anna, are you free Wednesday evening? I thought it might be nice if we had a dinner discussion for once. There's a nice little French bistro not far from here. Let me know and I'll book a table.

A joyful squawk, not unlike a seagull would make upon discovering a half-eaten packet of fish and chips, emitted from my lips. I left a suitable amount of time before I replied (six minutes and six seconds), then typed back in a flurry,

Hi Jeremy,

Yes, I'm free Wednesday evening. Ooh Italian, sounds wonderful, I'm totally up for it!

Can't wait,
Anna

I promptly deleted that message before I accidentally sent it. I sounded like a right eager beaver! No, the sensible thing to do would be to reply tomorrow morning and make him sweat all night, wondering what my answer would be.

But would that leave him enough time to book the table at the bistro? What if it filled up between now and tomorrow morning, and he decided that it was too much effort to book somewhere else and changed his mind? I knew I'd be kicking myself for not replying straightaway.

Fuck.

So I typed,

Yes, I'm free Wednesday evening. Sounds good,

Anna

Then I sent it before I could overthink it.

I had white fluffy clouds cushioning my feet as I walked home in the setting sun, hardly noticing the ache in my arches from wearing high heels all day.

Thomas was right: Jeremy did feel something. Our planets were aligning. Finally.

Underneath my elation was a small niggling worry that after reading about Mercy's disastrous supper with Jasper, I was setting myself up for the same disappointment. But it was a book written over two centuries ago. It had nothing whatsoever to do with me. This was simply sweet karma, gifting me for being patient and steadfast in my love.

My phone buzzed, and my stomach flipped when I saw it was Thomas. I was popular today.

TTTE: *Hey, do you want to meet up Wed night?*

Me: *Hi, so Jeremy invited me to dinner Wed night.*

TTTE: *Wow, what did you do?*

Me: *I may have worn a sexy little black dress to work.*

TTTE: *Lol. That will do it. Good to see old Jeremy has got* *eyes after all. Where is he taking you?*

Me: *French bistro.*

TTTE: *Oooh la la. So what about Tuesday then?*

Me: *Sorry can't, I'll be doing a complete body overhaul.*

TTTE: *Hahaha. I'd say that about one of my bikes but not about you. You look great Anna. Just be yourself.*

I released a deep breath. Maybe he was right. Why rush around like a headless chicken and stress myself out?

Me: OK, *thanks. That's reassuring. I was feeling exhausted by the thought of all the prep work.*

TTTE: *Trust me you're well prepped.*

I blushed a bit at that. I was thinking of what to say when another message popped up.

TTTE: *You'll be fine. This is what you want. Go get him! Message me if you need a pep talk on the night.*

I frowned. Thomas was being really good about this; he didn't have to give me moral support, but I was grateful all the same. Maybe he felt responsible since I knew Eleanor.

Me: *Are you sure?*

TTTE: *Yeah, I've got nothing else to do so I might as well make myself useful.*

Me: OK, *thanks, I know I'm going to be nervous.*

There was a part of me that wanted to see Thomas again, but I didn't think it was wise to fit him in for another practice session.

And Thomas, since he hadn't suggested meeting up tonight, obviously didn't think so either.

Chapter 14

I did not have to face Jasper the next morning, much to my relief. I had been dreading having to serve him coffee with Arabella's cries of ecstasy still ringing in my ears. Fortunately, he'd gone out early in his carriage, no doubt to run his lover home, so it was just Sebastian in the dining room.

'Would you like a roll, sir?' I asked him. He stared at me blankly for a second.

'A roll? Good heavens!'

'Yes, sir, a roll. Some bread?' I said, proffering a basket of freshly baked ones from Maggie's oven.

'Oh, a bread roll!' He laughed. 'For a second there, I thought you were propositioning me.'

'No, sir, I wasn't,' I said primly and plonked the basket on the table. 'Perhaps you should talk with Mr Donne about things like that and not make jokes with me.'

Sebastian stopped smiling and peered at me more closely. 'Are you feeling quite well today, Mercy? You look slightly peaky. Has Jasper said something to upset you? By Jove, I'll give him what for if he has!'

His kindness, as always, touched me. I was still so hurt by the events of last night that, to my embarrassment, a single tear overflowed and ran down my cheek. Sebastian was up like a shot.

'He has said something, that imbecile!' He put his arm around me and shepherded me over to the chair opposite. 'Now tell me, Mercy, what has my idiotic friend done? Was it something to do with that letter I gave you?'

I didn't know what to say. The idea of telling anyone seemed such a relief, but I couldn't bear Sebastian to know Jasper was toying with my affections and feel pity for me. So I nodded and briefly told him that Jasper had asked me to serve him and Arabella supper last night and that she had been none too polite to me.

'Ahh, I see,' said Sebastian. 'Yes, Arabella is beautiful, but deadly. She's Lord Bradnor's niece. He has an estate and grounds quite near here, and she visits him on occasion from London. She and Jasper became acquainted last spring, when Lord Bradnor invited us over to dine. They have since formed, shall we say, an *interesting* relationship. Personally, I can't see how he can stand her.'

'But she's so beautiful, sir. How could he not stand her?' I blurted.

Sebastian looked at me thoughtfully, as if grasping some

of my dilemma. 'She is nice to look at on the outside, but her character has some serious flaws that mar her truly being a beautiful person.'

'But how can a person with ... with outside flaws ever be seen as beautiful? How could anyone ever look past that when the flaws are so ...' My voice dropped to a whisper. 'Grotesque.' Sebastian squeezed my hand.

'I feel for you, child, I do. You've been given a heavy cross to bear, but bear it you must. You have strength and courage, and these will see you through. God knows your heart.'

At that, I buried my face in my hands and could not stifle my sobs. 'But, sir, what if no one ever sees me for who I am? What if I'm never loved but only despised?'

Sebastian grasped my shoulder tightly. 'Then you go on searching until you find someone who will love you and not despise you. There will be someone, I promise you. Unrequited love is not something I would wish on my worst enemy. Come now, dry your tears. That's the way. I have something that may be of use to you. Another book on Venice. Perhaps it will help you to read about a society that knows each other by who they are and not by seeing each other's faces, for they wear masks for some months of the year at the Carnevale.'

'Sir, I would like to live there if it meant people knowing

me without seeing my face.' I said this so solemnly that Sebastian chuckled.

'I'm sure you would, and myself also, but for other reasons of anonymity.'

He disappeared into his study and came out a few moments later. 'Here take this.' He handed me a slim green novel entitled *The Most Serene City of Masks*. 'And I'll ask Jasper to take care regarding who he invites for supper in future if he wants to stay here.'

'Oh, sir, no ...'

'I'll be discreet, don't worry, and you can be at ease. Jasper has enough to worry about without terrorising young maids.'

I wondered if he was referring to Jasper having to deal with being an orphan, but he didn't elaborate, and I didn't ask. I could only hope that he was right and that Jasper wouldn't carry on terrorising young maids.

*** *

I spent the morning downstairs busy with chores; and in the afternoon, as it was washing day tomorrow, I had to go upstairs to strip and remake the beds with fresh linen. I was hesitant to venture anywhere near Jasper's room after last night's performance, but I had no choice.

After I had completed my room and Sebastian's, I took a deep breath and pushed open Jasper's door. The room was even messier than it was the previous time. The bedclothes were mangled, as if a wrestling match had taken place. I sighed and started to strip the bed. Much to my dismay, in the midst of the bedclothes, I found a jewelled hairpin, a lace ribbon, and a silk stocking.

Shuddering, I threw them on the floor. Jasper could return them to their rightful owner himself. I was just tucking in the top coverlet when footsteps came up the stairs. Jasper, dressed in a black riding habit and carrying a whip, appeared in the doorway. He looked particularly striking this morning, and my heart skipped several beats. When he saw me making the bed, a slow smirk spread over his handsome face.

'Good, Mercy, you've righted the wrongs of my bedroom. Of course you can't erase the memory of them, but time heals all wounds.'

'Does it, sir?' I said, not looking up from plumping the pillows. 'I would've thought some wounds can never be healed.'

There was silence from the doorway. What was wrong with me? Why could I not hold my tongue lately?

But Jasper didn't scold me for impertinence. He came in, sat down in the easy chair, and flicked his whip idly.

'Indeed, Mercy, indeed.' Part of me could hardly believe we were actually having a cordial conversation. I'm afraid to say this rare courteousness from him made me bold, and the knowledge that I had about his past grew thick in my head. I wanted to somehow let him know that I knew, that I understood his pain, that he and I had both been scarred by the pox.

I gestured to the items I had thrown on the floor. 'Sir, I wasn't sure what to do with these. I-I'm guessing they are Miss Arabella's?'

Jasper yawned, showing off a perfect set of snowy-white teeth.

'Yes, they are. How very observant of you.'

I stepped closer to him. 'Sir, if I may say so, Miss is very beautiful. You ... you make a fine couple.' Jasper stared at me for a moment, then barked with laughter.

'I would like to say that means a lot to me, Mercy, but it doesn't. Arabella only wants one thing—well, two things if you count money in the equation.' I stepped even closer.

'Sir, then perhaps you should find someone who wants you for who you are.'

Jasper's expression turned bitter. 'And who would that be?'

By this time, I was standing so close to him that I could smell the spicy cologne he used and the sweat from his recent ride. I felt the urge to kiss him engulf me, and my feeling of love and compassion rose so quickly and strongly I was powerless to quell it.

As if he sensed what I was about to do, Jasper looked up, and our eyes locked. I read fear in their depths as he saw at close range my pockmarked face and all that meant to him. But he didn't tell me to go. I tentatively reached down and touched his hand lightly. His skin was soft and smooth. He quivered but didn't pull away.

'Someone who knows you, sir,' I whispered. 'Someone who ... knows.'

'What do you mean "knows"?' he breathed and grasped the whip more tightly in his other hand. 'Knows what exactly?'

I backed away. 'I ... Forgive me, sir. I spoke out of turn. I'll go now.'

But before I could leave, Jasper was out of the chair and rifling through the coats in the armoire. There was silence, and then he slammed the door. I almost jumped out of my skin. Fury had replaced fear in his eyes, and his lip curled in a snarl. 'Where is it? I know you have it, pox witch! I've caught you loitering around in here before, remember?'

I tried to tell myself fear was the catalyst to his outburst, but my heart stung at his name-calling. I backed away slowly, and he came towards me with his whip in his hand.

'Sir, I don't know what you mean.'

'Sir sir sir,' he mimicked. 'Always playing the innocent, aren't you? Well, perhaps I should teach you not to take things that aren't yours.'

I gulped. He sounded serious. Without waiting to hear another word, I wheeled around and fled the room. The last thing I heard as I headed for the stairs was Jasper screaming obscenities and mercilessly pounding the wall with his fist.

Chapter 15

There was nothing for it but to wear the same dress again on Wednesday. I had no time to go shopping, and it was the only sexy outfit I had. Plus I needed both nights to prepare my mind and body for 'the date'. On Monday night, I did a YouTube course in beginner's French because I knew Jeremy was fluent. I had some rudimentary knowledge from school, but I needed a refresher. Did I think he was going to expect me to converse in French? No. But I wanted to show I could parley-voo if required or at least nod my understanding. Then of course, there was the usual body prep, but forgoing the oily face mask (there was no way I wanted another repeat of Krakatoa).

While waxing my bikini line on Tuesday night, however, I wondered why I was bothering with that level of detail. I seriously doubted that anything sexual would be taking place even if Jeremy had been ogling me. *There's always Thomas*, I thought. *He'd appreciate it*. But despite enjoying Thomas's enthusiastic endeavours in the bedroom to get me up to speed, I wasn't sure if continuing our arrangement was a good idea. What if this date went well, and Jeremy and I started seeing each other outside of work on a regular basis? Being involved sexually with another guy would massively complicate things. But I enjoyed Thomas's company outside of the bedroom too. Perhaps he'd be amenable to being friends.

An image of him kissing my cheek and giving me *that look* swam into my mind as I ripped off the hardened wax with a grimace—somehow, I didn't think Thomas would like playing second fiddle to Jeremy.

By Wednesday afternoon, not surprisingly, I was a bundle of nerves and seriously considering popping to the nearest bar for a neat whisky shot or two.

Becca was giving me suspicious looks because of what I was wearing. 'Why are you so dressed up again?' she asked.

'I'm going to the opera with my mother. She's been visiting from London for a few days,' I said with conviction.

'Ah, I see.' Becca knew from my mother's previous expeditions to Oxford that she could be exacting. Luckily, she didn't ask me what opera we were seeing as I had no idea what was on.

Speaking of my mother, her Saturday night invite loomed in the distance—the night where I would have to spend an awkward evening in the company of my sister and my ex, pretending I was over their betrayal. Maybe if Jeremy was starting to think of me in a romantic sense, he wouldn't mind accompanying me to London. The look on my sister's face when I turned up with him in tow would be sweet karma indeed.

Unfortunately, sweet karma didn't extend to the weather. Grey clouds gathered and the sky darkened outside my office window. Jeremy had confirmed that he'd meet me outside after work and we'd walk there. But as the afternoon progressed and translucent droplets ran down the windowpane, I worried he might decide it was all too hard and call it off. Silence ensued, and I waited on tenterhooks, my armpits wet with anxiety.

Just as I was about to lose my mind, he messaged, saying he'd pick me up out front and we'd drive to the restaurant. The tightness in my gut eased. He was a pro at this; all I had to do was relax and enjoy his company, along with some excellent French food and wine. There was nothing to tie myself in knots about.

It was raining heavily when I opened the main door of the building and poked my head out. There was no sign of Jeremy's car, and I didn't want to stand out in this without an umbrella. Unless he was parked farther along and I couldn't see him? Shit.

Unbuckling my trench, I held it over my head and tottered down the puddle-strewn path to the front gate. No car. I didn't have his mobile number, so I couldn't text him. After an indeterminable wait under a dripping tree, his black MINI Cooper pulled up with a flourish next to the waterlogged kerb; and I jumped back, narrowly missing getting splashed from head to foot. The passenger door sprung open, and I collapsed inside, bundling my coat in front of me. But it effectively sent a rivulet of water all down my stockings. I banged the door shut, muttering an expletive.

'Hi,' said Jeremy, sounding amused. A quick glance over and I saw he was unruffled in a black raincoat with the collar turned up, his hair slightly damp. A grin on his handsome face. The space suddenly seemed too small for the both of us, and I found it hard to breathe. Was there a phobia for being in a car with a searingly hot guy?

'Bit wet out there, huh? Would you like a towel?'

'Yes, please,' I squeaked, feeling drips wandering down my neck and wondering about the state of my mascara.

'Sorry I took so long. There was a queue in the parking lot. Excuse me.' Jeremy reached in front of me to open the passenger glovebox, his arm briefly brushing mine, and handed me a small folded blue hand towel. It smelt of old perfume. Did his dates use it to dry off if they got too hot and sweaty in his presence? I dabbed it perfunctorily on my décolletage and placed it to one side. I'd sort myself out once we got to the bistro.

'So bonjour, comment allez-vous?' I said brightly as

Jeremy put on his blinker and pulled away from the kerb. Might as well show off my conversational French skills.

'Ah, très bien, merci,' he replied, checking his side mirror. 'I didn't know you spoke French?'

'Un peu,' I said, feeling glad I'd made the effort and done that YouTube course. Now I was setting myself apart from those random women he dated.

But then Jeremy rattled off an incomprehensible sentence that ended with a question mark and glanced at me expectantly.

I gulped. That was a bit beyond beginner's level.

'Er, oui, bien sûr,' I replied, not knowing what else to say.

But it seemed to be the right answer because he smiled widely. 'Parfait! Nous pouvons faire ça.'

Oh great. What had I just agreed to? Hopefully, it was something pleasant, like going to Paris with him.

We arrived at the restaurant—a rather austere, but chic space with sconce lighting, wooden floorboards, and modern seating. I was expecting French-type artwork or photos on the wall to set the atmosphere, but there were none. Jeremy had assured me, however, that the food was good. He seemed to come here regularly. While I headed to the ladies' to sort out my hair and face, Jeremy said he'd order our starters.

When I returned, feeling marginally less bedraggled, I found a small white plate on my side of the table with a pair of round tongs and a two-pronged fork resting beside it. There was also an opened bottle of red wine and two glasses poured. Jeremy was currently swigging from one. As I sat down, a waiter appeared and served us both silver dishes filled with half a dozen gently steaming brown shells.

I looked at the dish in alarm. Snails! Urgh!

Jeremy set his wine down and picked up his tongs. 'I couldn't believe it when you said "oui" in the car as no one I ever bring here wants me to order them snails.'

Oh god. This was obviously something he really enjoyed. Snails were a French delicacy after all, and this was my chance to impress him.

I forced a smile and inclined my head towards the dish. A waft of garlic and a faint earthy smell hit my nostrils, and my stomach churned. Following his lead, I grasped a snail in my tongs and used the fork to dig out a fleshy grey slug.

'Bon appétit!' Jeremy said enthusiastically and popped it in his mouth. There was nothing for it but to put the slug in my own mouth and chew. It tasted like tyre rubber basted with garlic and had a lingering aftertaste of soil. I quickly washed it down with a large gulp of wine.

Worried he was going to order us frog legs next, I

grabbed the leather-bound menu and said, 'I'll check out the mains.'

'I'm paying for this, by the way. So don't hold back. Get the filet mignon if you like. I am.' Jeremy popped another snail in his mouth and patted his glistening lips delicately with a napkin. I stared, feeling slightly lustful. Trust Jeremy to make ingesting snails look sexy.

After I'd forced down another couple of snails and several more large gulps of wine, I was beginning to feel pleasantly tipsy, if a little nauseous from eating slugs. But I was relieved the date was going well. Jeremy talked mostly about his book, which he'd started writing. But that was OK; it was inherently interesting to me. This was why I loved him—what other man would get so excited about smallpox outbreaks?

He wiped his hands on a napkin. 'Have you finished that memoir yet? I was thinking I'd quite like to read it after all.'

My gut hopped. I wondered what Jeremy would make of Jasper bonking Arabella while Mercy cowered in bed having to listen to it. Then there was the latest encounter in his room involving her hasty escape before he pounded the wall with his fist. The guy was a first-class bully. Couldn't she see how horrible he was? I wanted to reach into the past and shake some sense into her. Plus I didn't want Jeremy reading anything about unrequited love at this point in time.

He might start seeing similarities.

'Honestly, it's a bit rambly and all over the place. I can send you through my notes when I'm finished to save you the effort,' I countered. 'The majority of it is her coping with life after smallpox. The scarring made things a struggle.'

Jeremy tutted. 'That is unfortunate. Any mention of vision loss?'

'No.' However, maybe there was if Mercy had seen herself reflected in the cloche as scar-free and perfect. Poor thing.

Jeremy started talking about a lecture he was giving next week, and I nodded along but felt a little impatient. When was he going to ask me anything personal? Didn't he want to know about my hobbies or my friends? I'd thought we'd get to know each other.

I started to feel uneasy—was this a working dinner and not a date after all?

When I'd met Thomas, he'd defined our encounter straightaway as a date, and I'd liked that. It gave me a solid brick wall to lean against. I knew what was going on. This dinner with Jeremy felt flimsy, like tissue paper.

That is, until we both reached for the salt to sprinkle on our filet mignons and knocked over the entire pot. There was much laughter and scooping up of salt from the table.

In the confusion, Jeremy took the chance to deliberately entwine his salty fingers with mine. I nearly spontaneously combusted.

OK, so it wasn't a working dinner?

I looked down at our meshed fingers and back up at him, hardly able to believe he was touching me—finally. The corner of his mouth quirked. 'Now we have to throw it over our left shoulders,' he said, rubbing his thumb lazily against mine. 'Or it's bad luck.'

'Ah, right. That is the superstition, isn't it?' I said, his touch feeling like the sun on a winter's day.

'It's the left shoulder because that's apparently where the devil sits,' he continued, squeezing my fingers. 'Throwing salt in his eyes keeps him away.'

'Fascinating,' I said, squeezing his fingers back. 'I wonder where that originated from.'

'The Last Supper. Judas Iscariot spilled the salt cellar.'

Together, we threw pinches of salt over our left shoulders, and I hoped I hit the devil right in the eyes with mine. I didn't want any interference in what was now looking to be an actual date with Jeremy.

We returned to our food, having salted our respective filet mignons. After finishing my meal, I made an excuse to go to the ladies', leaving him perusing the dessert menu. Clutching the edge of the counter, I took a few deep breaths to calm down. My heart was jumping around in my chest like the Energizer Bunny. Just as I thought it was one thing, he'd completely upped the ante, and now it was another. What would happen after dinner? I had no idea.

But if he was holding my hand, there was a possibility of him being up for something else later. Maybe at least a kiss? That was both exciting and nerve-wracking.

I used the loo, checked my phone, and saw I had a message from Thomas.

TTTE: *How's the date going?*

Me: *Good!*

TTTE: *Has he made a move yet?*

Me: *Yes! He held my hand.*

TTTE: *Great (thumbs up emoji). Sounds like he's into you.*

Me: *I hope so. But I'm nervous about what's going to happen after dinner. What if he wants to kiss me? Should I let him or play hard to get?*

TTTE: *How long have you been in love with this guy?*

Me: *Just over two years.*

TTTE: *I really don't think you should play hard to get.*

Me: *Right. Thanks for the advice.*

TTTE: *No problem. Message me later if you get stuck.*

Me: *I think I should be fine.*

TTTE: *OK. Have fun!*

***

With Thomas's words of encouragement playing on my mind, I was only too happy to acquiesce with a 'oui!' when Jeremy suggested we take a detour to his place after the crème brûlée. He said he had an 'artefact' that he thought I might find interesting and that he'd drop me back at my flat afterwards.

I imagined it was a line he'd used many times before. But now that he was using it on me, I wasn't complaining. Since we were headed to his house, I was pretty sure that he had more in mind than just a kiss. Thank goodness I'd had that practise with Thomas, or I'd be a nervous wreck right now.

As it was, one of my legs had developed a nervous tremor, and my stomach kept clenching whenever I thought about it.

The rain had eased off, and the sky was clearing as we reached the outskirts of town and started passing hedgerows and fields with round golden bales of hay. It was still relatively light as we'd clocked over to daylight savings the weekend before.

'Gosh, this is a bit of a hike into town each day,' I commented.

'It is a little,' Jeremy replied, concentrating on the road, which had narrowed considerably. 'My wife and I bought the house as a kind of country retreat.'

I gave a start. *Wife!*

He coughed. 'I should say *ex-wife*. We're divorced.'

My heart rate lowered from its adrenaline spike. 'I didn't realise you'd been married.'

'Yeah,' he said with a sigh. 'Not something I'm looking to repeat anytime soon. The rectory has become a millstone around my neck. I'll probably sell it at some point.'

I whipped my head around. 'Rectory?'

'Yes, it's been converted. Well, partly. We bought it as a doer-upper, but it's grade II listed. So there's a ton of things you can't do. It's more of a don'ter-upper.' He chuckled at his own joke.

'How long have you lived there?'

'About four years.'

I couldn't believe it. He lived in a rectory. What were the chances? Hopefully, he didn't have a whip as well!

Not too long after, we drove up a gravelled driveway to a two-storey white-brick house covered with ivy. It was like something off a chocolate box.

'There you go. Small, but perfectly formed—just how I like my women,' Jeremy quipped.

Cheesy, I thought. But at least he was attempting to flirt.

'It looks lovely,' I said, peering through the rain-smeared windscreen.

'Let's go in. I'll put the kettle on and show you the artefact. I think it's something you'll like.'

Oh yes, the *artefact*. I grinned to myself, wondering if it would resemble the clay specimen I'd lovingly crafted. Thomas's face, his eyes closed in pleasure, popped unbidden into my mind. Dammit, I shouldn't have replied to his message. This wasn't the time to be thinking about handling *his* artefact!

'You'll have to excuse the muddle. I'm still sorting things out from a recent antique haul,' Jeremy said, turning his key in the white-painted door.

'Don't worry,' I said, following him in. 'I do a bit of antique shopping myself.'

I was expecting a few vases or some such to be lying around. But the sight that met my eyes when we passed by the lounge was more than a few vases. It appeared that Jeremy hadn't shopped for the odd item—he'd practically bought the whole store! I paused and stared.

The low-ceilinged room with oak beams was stuffed to the brim. Grandfather clocks, tables holding crockery and china, cabinets jammed with glassware, boxes of knick-knacks, framed paintings propped on chairs, and books (so many books) stacked everywhere. You couldn't see the floor. Well, you could see a small corner of a Turkish rug, but that was it.

Jeremy abruptly pulled the door shut, and I felt relieved the mess was hidden. 'As I said, I'm still sorting things out. Kitchen is this way.' He sounded a bit embarrassed.

'Oh, right.'

I followed him down a narrow hallway with blue-flowered wallpaper to the back of the house. *The kitchen must be the tidy sanctuary where he hangs out,* I thought. But upon reaching the kitchen, I was disconcerted to see that it wasn't a sanctuary or tidy in the slightest. There was a leaning tower of dirty plates in the sink, open pizza boxes on the table, various electronics, stuff all over the bench, and a general feeling of fusty grime.

Jeremy swept the pizza boxes off the table and dumped

them by the overflowing bin. He gestured for me to sit down while he switched on the kettle. I picked my way across the sticky floor, avoiding a brown sauce-like stain that had been oozing its way across but had since dried and hardened.

'Tea?' Jeremy asked.

I nodded mutely.

'White?' He opened the fridge to get out the milk, and a distinct smell of rotting vegetables hit my nostrils.

'Black is fine, thanks,' I said faintly, trying not to breathe in the fumes.

Feeling a bit shocked, I looked around as it slowly sunk in. Jeremy actually lived like this. Should I say something? Or ignore the white elephant in the room? Part of me was a bit annoyed that he'd invited me round when his house was so untidy. Even if he hated housework, surely, he could've made an effort? I wasn't a clean freak by any means (OK, I was a little bit of a clean freak). But if he'd been coming to mine, I would've at least done the dishes and put out the rubbish. Even Thomas's flat was better than this, *and* his loo was passably clean for a guy.

But what could I say? This was the man I cared about; and if you loved someone, weren't you meant to accept them, warts and all?

Jeremy bustled around at the sink, sourcing mugs and

cleaning them out. How could he look so groomed and exist in utter shambles? He was a walking dichotomy.

Bringing over our mugs of hot tea, he sat down opposite. I tentatively took a small sip. I was reluctant to drink too much in case I needed the loo. Something told me Jeremy's toilet might not be that hygienic.

I tried to be diplomatic and kind.

'How has it been living here since you separated from your wife?' I asked.

'A bit up and down, to tell you the truth.' He scratched his forehead. 'I found it really tough at first.'

'Why did you break up? If you don't mind me asking.'

Jeremy smiled ruefully. 'In her words, "I didn't sign up to live with a slob".' He glanced around the kitchen. 'I mean, I know I'm a little messy. But it's not too bad, is it?'

I gulped. OK, so this was a major issue.

'It's a little lived-in. Maybe you could hire a weekly cleaner,' I said gently (or like five of them and pronto). 'I can help you arrange it.'

He gave me a lopsided grin, and my heart throbbed for him despite his disgusting kitchen.

'Thanks, Anna. You're the best. Drink up, and I'll show you that artefact. It's in my bedroom.'

Chapter 16

Maggie required me to run errands in town after I came downstairs, so I was able to vacate the rectory. If she noticed my wild eyes and skittish manner, she didn't comment on it.

I shrugged on my cloak, grabbed my basket, and practically ran from the house. Halfway down the path, I turned back to look up at Jasper's window and thought I saw a curtain twitch. *Let him watch me,* I thought. Hopefully, he felt contrite about scaring me half to death in that uncalled-for manner. Yes, I had stolen his letter, but to scream and rant and pound the wall were the actions of a madman. For the first time, I considered that Jasper might actually be insane. Could I truly be in love with such a person?

My errands in town took no time at all; and though it was freezing cold, I lingered at each, drawing out the time when I would have to go back to the rectory. Any time not spent in the same house as Jasper was preferable.

It was almost dusk when I reluctantly turned to go back. To draw out my journey even further, I decided to take the long way through the woods that bordered the back of the town and eventually joined up with the rectory. I had been through once before, so I knew there was a clear path and that I should easily be able to find my way home.

The fading light did not bother me, and I felt at ease as I trod the well-worn track. The solid oak trees soothed my frazzled nerves, and the late-afternoon sunlight filtered down through the treetops, piercing the cold gloom.

However, underneath the sound of my steps, I became aware of movement—a kind of scuffling noise. I looked behind me but could see nothing. I quickened my pace. There it was again. Something or someone was following me. With my heart racing, I started to run, the basket of food heavy in my arms.

Eventually, though, I could run no further and backed up against a tree, pausing for breath. *Let whatever it is attack me,* I thought. *Better that than being afraid.* I stood and waited, hardly daring to breathe.

Then right in front of me, a gypsy man appeared. I felt the urge to scream but bit my tongue. Dusk was now falling, so I could only make out that he wore mud-stained breeches, a dirty waistcoat and shirt and had an old blanket wrapped around him. His face was hidden by a black hat with a wide brim. In his hand, he held a butcher's knife, which he now brought up towards me. I stiffened in terror.

He spoke not a word but came closer until I felt the warmth of his body. His breath smelt rank and I shrank back as he pulled down the hood of my cloak and proceeded to sniff my hair. I was glad of the ensuing darkness, for it meant he could not see my face properly. Even though he was a gypsy, I still had my pride. If I was about to be ravaged, at least let him think I was beautiful.

At this point, I had not had a good look at my attacker, but now I saw him properly. And the face was not male; it had high cheekbones, rosebud-red lips, and creamy skin streaked with grime. Bright green eyes, fringed with dark lashes, looked into mine with a bitter expression.

'Miss, please let me go ... Take my money ... some food. Just please let me go. My master will be getting worried and come looking for me.'

The girl spat violently into the ground beside me and stabbed her knife into the tree trunk above my head. She was about my age, but a good deal taller than me.

'Master, eh? Does he treat you good?' she snarled, her red lips curling in a sneer. 'Or does he make you do chores after everyone else has gone to bed? Extra-special chores.'

'I ... I don't know what you mean. He's a good man. He's a rector.'

The girl laughed uproariously at this. 'A rector! The worst of all.'

She peered intently into my face, raking my pox scars with her gaze. 'Be grateful you've had that which makes men leave you alone. If I could have anything, I'd wish for the Speckled Monster to claim me.'

I was amazed—trade in her beauty for my ugliness? She must be half crazed with hunger. I thrust my basket at her. 'Here, take anything you want. Please let me go now.'

The girl searched through the basket. Her mouth quivered as she took out a loaf of freshly baked bread, a soft cheese, and a couple of ripe apples. She looked at me, and her expression softened.

'Thank you. I am very hungry. I left my place of employment last week, and I haven't eaten much, as you can imagine.'

Before I could stop myself, I said, 'You should come with me back to the rectory. You could have a wash and a proper meal.'

As if realising what a mess she must look and how badly she must smell, the girl self-consciously smoothed her hair and plucked at her shirt.

'Alright,' she said suddenly. 'Yes, I will come. That is very kind of you to offer.' She put the food back into my basket and lifted it onto her hip. 'Lead on to the rectory by all means. My name's Rose, by the way. Rose Baker.'

'Mercy Graham. Pleased to make your acquaintance.'

By the time we reached the rectory, it was dark and very cold. Once I'd managed to locate the back door, I brought Rose into the warm kitchen to get her some food. To my surprise, Jasper was there and having what looked like a heated discussion with Maggie. When we walked in, they stopped speaking and stared at us.

Maggie recovered first and came forward, wiping her hands on her apron, her face red and flustered.

'Mercy, we was getting worried about you! You've been away some while! And who's this you've got with you?'

I looked at Jasper warily. His handsome face didn't look worried; it looked livid. He glanced at Rose and gave her the once-over. Dressed as a man and covered in grime, she still radiated an ethereal beauty.

'This is Rose. I found her starving in the woods,' I said pointedly; and Maggie, as I knew she would, hustled us to the table and started loading a couple of plates with hot beef stew.

My stomach was gripped with a gnawing hunger, and I was so concerned with eating my stew that I forgot Jasper was still there until he slammed his fist down on the table so hard our plates jumped a foot in the air.

He glared at me fiercely, and I felt the hairs on the back of my neck stand to attention. He leaned forward menacingly across the table and growled, 'I know you have it, pox! Don't play the innocent maid with me!' Then he swept from the room rather dramatically.

Rose looked at me, her eyes wide with shock. 'Who the blooming heck was that?'

If I hadn't been so petrified, I would've laughed at the expression on her face. I tried to shrug nonchalantly, but I was shaking in my boots

'Oh, don't mind Mr Donne,' said Maggie airily, stirring something briskly on the stove. 'His bark's worse than 'is bite. He's got some fool notion that you've stolen some letter of 'is, Mercy. Wanted me to search your room until whatever he's lost was found. Being quite demanding he was just now, but I stood my ground. "Miss Mercy's a good girl," I told him. "She would no' take what's no' hers."'

I gulped down a chunk of bread and tried to look innocent. Rose glanced at me, and I blushed. She grinned approvingly. 'Not such a good girl after all,' her expression seemed to say.

Meanwhile, Maggie had moved on to a more interesting topic. 'So, Miss Rose, where are you from?'

She looked curiously at Rose's outfit and her obvious hunger; she was shovelling food into her mouth like there was no tomorrow. Perhaps in her mind, this would be the last meal she would have for a while. My heart contracted in pity. What had happened to make this girl choose the life of a common thief?

Rose eventually stopped chewing, and the story came out. She had been working at Lord Bradnor's manor up until last week as a scullery maid. Her job was to help the cook by preparing vegetables and washing dishes, as well as other duties such as lighting the fires in the dining room, drawing room, and main bedrooms. Apparently, Lord Bradnor had come across her clearing out the ashes in his bedroom fireplace and had tried to accost her.

'He had his hand up my skirt when his wife walked in. It didn't look too good from where she was standing. I was instantly dismissed without the wages I was owed for the last month. I had nowhere to go. My family lives up north, and I had no money to get there. After a night of almost freezing to death in the woods with only a small blanket, I decided if I didn't do something drastic, I would die. So I stole these clothes and a knife, and I've been holding people at knifepoint until they give me money or food. Oh, I don't hurt them,' she said hurriedly, seeing Maggie's alarmed face. 'I just scare them a little. Mercy here is the first one who's offered me a proper meal, though.'

I was riveted by Rose's story. I couldn't imagine being so alone and desperate that you were forced into being a criminal.

'But, child, why didn't you turn to the parish? Father Fannon would've helped you without question,' said Maggie. Rose scowled and looked as if she wanted to spit.

'The church and I don't exactly get along,' she said, looking shifty. I sensed there was more to the story, but Maggie didn't press her.

'Well, you're here now,' she said briskly. 'And upon my honour as a Christian, I'll not turn out someone in need of food or shelter. I'll talk to Father Fannon and see if we can find you a few jobs around here in exchange for a decent meal and a bed. You can share with Mercy for now.'

Later, when we were safely ensconced upstairs in my room and getting ready for bed, Rose asked me about Jasper, as I knew she would. I could tell she was burning with curiosity.

'So he's some kind of upper-crust, but he's living here and coming and going as he pleases? Sounds a little odd to me. Why don't he have any family?'

'He does,' I said, brushing my hair a little too vigorously. 'An uncle. But he seems to prefer living here with Sebastian. He's studying at Oxford, and he's travelled a lot.'

'Oh, has he?' said Rose, throwing back the covers and hopping into bed. She had given her face and feet a thorough scrubbing at my washbasin, but the rest of her was still a bit grimy. I hoped she kept well over on her side of the bed.

'You seem to know him quite well,' she continued, 'despite the fact he looked ready to murder you in the kitchen. You have got it, haven't you? Whatever it is that he's missing?'

I slid into bed and lay still. If truth be told, the burden of the letter was becoming more than I could bear. But I didn't know how much Rose could be trusted with my secret: that I loved Jasper so passionately that my heart was breaking in two. She would probably laugh herself silly if I told her. In the end, I compromised.

'Yes, I have got it, but I didn't know it meant that much to him.' A small white lie. 'I was being nosey. But things got out of hand, and now I don't know how to rectify them.' Another white lie. I could easily put the letter back.

'So what does it say?' she asked.

'What does what say?'

She snorted. 'The letter, silly. What does it say in the letter?'

'Oh, nothing too exciting. Just inheritance guff. He must need it to claim his fortune or something.' I yawned. 'Anyway, I'll give it back to him, and he'll leave me alone. Let's stop talking and go to sleep. I'm tired.'

I snuffed out the candle, and the subject was dropped. Little did I know that in the coming days, Rose's time in the woods proved to give her the strength and determination to deal with a situation very different from my own.

Chapter 17

How do I get myself into these situations? I wondered. *Do I have 'gullible' written on my forehead in invisible ink?*

At this point in time, Jeremy was undressing and expecting me to come back from the bathroom, ready for a session of horseplay—and I was to be the horse.

The 'artefact' had turned out to be a tortoiseshell-handled riding whip. Surprise, surprise. My life was starting to mirror Mercy's to the point I could practically predict what was going to happen to me.

'Circa 1740 to 1750,' Jeremy had said when he'd brought it out from his top dresser drawer. 'Look at the workmanship.' He'd turned it over in his hand, showing me. The silver mount had a Rococo scroll and flowers.

'It's a lovely piece,' I'd said politely (naively, as it turned out).

'Yes, I thought we could have a bit of fun with it.'

'Huh?'

'You know.' He'd reached around and tapped me lightly on the behind, and I'd drawn a sharp breath. Taking my shocked silence for excitement, he'd started unbuttoning his shirt. I'd muttered an excuse about needing the loo and scuttled off down the hallway, nearly breaking my ankle when I'd kicked over a pile of old newspapers.

Standing in the middle of his grimy bathroom (I was right—the toilet needed serious disinfecting before I could be enticed to use it), I hovered on the fence.

Apart from the fact that Jeremy's bedroom was as unkempt as the rest of his house, expecting me to frolic around naked while he whipped my backside was taking things a bit far. But then again, if I turned him down flat, he probably wouldn't offer any kind of intimacy again. This could be my first and only date with him.

I had no idea what to do.

Fuck it.

I rang Thomas before I could chicken out. It was either him or Isabel, and I knew she'd laugh more than offer helpful advice.

He answered on the second ring. 'Hey! What's up?'

'I need some help,' I said in a low whisper, tucking my chin into my chest so my voice wouldn't carry.

'What's going on? Where are you?' Thomas asked, his tone laced with concern.

'Bathroom. Slight problem. Jeremy wants to whip me with his eighteenth-century riding crop.'

There was a crackle as the mouthpiece was covered, but I could still hear the sound of muffled chortling.

'It's not funny! I need advice!'

Thomas came back on the line after a few seconds. 'Well, the question is, do you want to get *neigh-ked* with him?' His voice brimmed with mirth. 'You just have to say yay or *neigh*.' He made a whinnying noise, but I was in no mood for jokes.

'Thomas! Honestly, this is serious. What should I do?' I paced around in my heels, trying to keep away from a grubby-looking towel that had been left strewn on the floor to fester.

'Sorry, I couldn't help it. Look, the fact that he's wanting to role-play is a good thing, right?'

'No!' I hissed. 'It's moving too fast. I need to work up to that sort of stuff.'

'You seemed fine with the vibrator ...'

'That was different. I'd had a few drinks, and it just sort of progressed naturally. I can't go from drinking a cup of tea in the kitchen to being whipped in the bedroom five minutes later.'

'Ah. Well, you best take control of the situation then. Try to slow things down so you feel more comfortable.'

'How?'

'Maybe give him a massage.'

I wasn't sure if I was confident enough to give Jeremy a full-body massage. I'd once given my ex-boyfriend, Ben, one; and he hadn't been complimentary or asked for one again. I wasn't sure what I'd done wrong as we hadn't discussed things like that. Probably part of the reason he'd run off with my sister.

'What about a foot rub?' I suggested. 'Or is that too weird?'

'Oooh yes. I'm sure he'd *love* that,' Thomas said, sounding wistful, as if he might quite like one himself.

'Well, OK. Thanks,' I said, glad to have some sort of game plan. 'And sorry for bothering you.'

'No problem. Good luck, and if he gets impatient, tell him to hold his horses!'

When I re-entered Jeremy's bedroom, I was disconcerted to see him lying under the bedcovers with his hands locked behind his head and, judging from his bare chest, obviously naked. For some reason, I'd pictured his chest to be smooth and hairless like Thomas's, but it was covered with thick brown hair and looked a lot like a bear pelt. It wasn't a problem. I was just taken aback. Who knew *that* had been hiding under his shirt?

'Who were you talking to in the bathroom?' he asked.

'Oh, er, my mother.' She was being used as an excuse a

lot today. Her ears would be burning.

Jeremy looked me over, his gaze lingering on my boobs.

'Do you need help with your zipper?'

My eyes flicked to the whip that was resting on his bedside table and panicked. 'I ... I thought maybe I could give you a foot rub before ... anything else.'

Jeremy's eyes shifted to the end of the bed, then swivelled back to me. 'Okaaaay, I guess so. There's some lotion in here somewhere.' He leaned over and opened the bedside drawer, pulling out a box of condoms labelled 'Magnum BareSkin' and placing it on top. 'For later,' he said, winking at me, and I gulped. Why did I suddenly feel like I was one in a long line of women?

He handed me a bottle of moisturising lotion. Right! I perched on the end of the bed and pulled up the end of the duvet to expose his feet. So Jeremy's face was bordering on perfection. His feet—not so much. They were large and bony with strange knobbly toes, and the skin on the heels was dry and cracked.

I didn't want to be judgemental. It wasn't like I was a supermodel, but I did put a lot of effort into grooming myself from top to toe before any kind of meeting with him (doubly intensive for this date). Yet it seemed he didn't think it necessary to do the same.

But I'd said I would give him a foot rub, so I supposed I

had to go through with it. When I thought back to all my daydreaming about what it would be like going on a date with Jeremy, I wanted to burst out laughing. Massaging his manky feet had never once featured in the scenario.

I squirted a liberal amount of lotion on one foot and half-heartedly did a few swirls on his instep.

Jeremy sighed. 'That feels nice. My ex-wife used to massage my feet.'

'Oh, did she?' I felt a bit better that I was reminding him of his wife and started to think of this as more like a project. Instead of working on his book, I was now working on his feet. It was an easy transition and a good bonding experience for us. The first of many evenings we would spend together ...

'Yes, before we got married,' Jeremy continued, now placing his hands on his hairy chest. 'Ours was a bit of a whirlwind romance. Perhaps that's why things fell apart after only a year. It's been ... hard. We tried getting back together once or twice, but it didn't work. Along with the whole cleaning thing, apparently, I have some idiosyncrasies that annoy her.'

My eyes flicked to the whip.

'Really?' I said nervously. I did some stroking up his ankle and then around his knobbly toes.

'Yes, I guess that's why I always go out with women

once or twice now—I can't seem to commit to anyone after her.' He laughed self-deprecatingly. 'It's a failing, I know, and I suppose I should go to a therapist.' He shrugged. 'But they'll tell me what she told me: I'm too selfish.'

'That's a bit harsh,' I said, rubbing my knuckles down the side of his foot. 'Maybe you haven't met the right person ... The One.'

'Nah, I don't believe in that rubbish,' he scoffed. 'The One? That's a fairytale.'

'Oh.'

'Besides, now that I'm back on the market, I find I quite like sex with a lot of different women. Mind you, I've never brought anyone back here. I usually have sex with them in my car or go to theirs, so you're a bit special.'

I balked at that, remembering the hand towel and how it stunk of stale perfume. Ick. But he'd called me 'special'. That was something at least? I did some thumb sweeps on his arch, but his comment about having sex with random women in his car was too hard to ignore and really off-putting. The foot massage was a bad idea; it was making him relax and open up to me, and I wasn't liking what I was hearing.

Plus, for some reason, my mind kept wandering to Thomas. It must've been because I'd just spoken to him. The horse puns *were* quite funny. And I did enjoy our practice sessions. He made me feel sexy, yet comfortable, and he didn't mention using whips. Plus he was hot ...

'Anna, are you listening?'

I'd been making vague patting motions with my hand while Jeremy was warbling away.

'Hmm, sorry?'

'I said if we're going to have a one-off tonight, you need to keep it hush-hush afterwards.'

I lifted my hand off his foot entirely.

'What?'

Jeremy made a zipping motion across his lips. 'I don't want it getting around that I sleep with my staff. However, as soon as you walked into my office in that dress, I knew, on this occasion, I was willing to make an exception. But it might be a good idea not to wear it again. Go back to your normal attire so I'm not tempted.' He chuckled.

Wow. He had some nerve telling me what to wear. And this was a one-off?

It seemed it had never entered his head that there was going to be another date. I would indeed be one in a long line of forgettable women for him—even if I could hold my own in a conversation about smallpox.

The veil partially lifted, and I got a flash of who he really was: a handsome slob with commitment issues. And it all felt extremely wrong, me being there.

'I'm sorry, I can't do this. I think I'm going to leave.' I wiped my sticky hands on the cover and moved towards the edge of the bed. 'Don't get up. I'll book an Uber.'

In the end, after multiple failed attempts to locate an Uber or get hold of a taxi, Jeremy got dressed while I waited in the kitchen; and he drove me home. The conversation on the way was awkward and stilted. He parked outside my flat.

'Good night, Anna,' he said in a clipped tone, as if he was embarrassed or I'd inconvenienced him—I wasn't sure which. He didn't attempt to kiss me good night, even on the cheek. Jeremy, his house, the whole evening, in fact, had completely bewildered me.

The only bright spot was my conversation with Thomas, which had me giggling to myself in the shower as I washed off the grungy feeling of being in Jeremy's dirty home and, surprisingly, of touching him.

* * *

At work the next day, I was still going over the whole thing in my mind. It was so weird and slightly bizarre. The Jeremy of last night wasn't matching with the image I had been cherishing inside my head. What had happened to the Jeremy I loved? Surely, he still existed?

On my way to the kitchen to grab a coffee, I veered past his office with the intention of clearing the air. Before I could think too much about it, I knocked, and Jeremy said, 'Come in.'

I had my speech already planned, something along the lines of 'Maybe we should try that again ...' But I found that he wasn't alone. A slim blonde girl was sitting in my chair. She and Jeremy broke off from some kind of intense discussion when I entered. My heart sank as I recognised her. Irish Lucy—even more beautiful and bosomy in the flesh, wearing a scoop-necked black-and-white polka-dot dress with a slit up the side. God, he'd be loving that!

'Sorry, I can come back later,' I said, turning to go, but Jeremy waved me in.

'Anna, this is Lucy Flanagan. We were about to finish up, but I think it went really well.'

'You do? Oh, great,' said Lucy, simpering at him. 'And thank you so much for the coffee. I adore espresso.'

'Glad to hear it,' said Jeremy, grinning. 'Well, I've got one other interview, but I'll be in touch as soon as possible to let you know the outcome.'

Lucy beamed, her blue eyes sparkling, and I clenched my fists. I hated her already. How was I going to bear sharing an office with her?

'Did you want to discuss something, Anna?' Jeremy

asked, but I couldn't speak. If last night wasn't bad enough, now he was interviewing someone who was going to worm her way into his affections any chance she got. It was like he wanted to put me in one of those medieval torture devices and twist the screws.

'No, it's fine. It can wait,' I said, gritting my teeth.

'Nice to meet you, Anna. Hopefully, see you again,' Lucy said with a knowing look.

I turned on my heel and left them to it. It was a done deal. He was going to hire her—I just knew it.

Fuming, I went back to my office, strode over to the waste paper basket, and kicked it as hard as I could across the room. Then I had to bend down and collect all the scrunched-up bits of paper that had come flying out of it.

Becca stared at me as if I'd gone mad. 'What's with you? Did they run out of chocolate digestives?'

I sat down and grabbed hold of my mouse, bringing up the faculty vacancies page. 'You were right. I think I should look for another position—something with better pay and a female boss.'

Becca didn't ask anything else, but I heard her say quietly under her breath, 'You go, girl.'

After firing off several job applications with my CV attached, I felt slightly better, if still a little manic. Jeremy was about to make my life hell, so the least I could do was make his life uncomfortable too, namely by removing myself from his project. Let Lucy edit and footnote his blasted smallpox book. While I was at it, why not schedule in some extra practice sessions with Thomas? Fuck it, why not invite him to my mother's house?

Me: *Hi, I know this is out of the blue but would you be interested in coming to London with me on Saturday afternoon? It's a family dinner at my mother's flat in Bayswater. I'm warning you, it could be a shit show. My sister and my ex will be there. And we'd have to stay overnight.*

Thomas messaged back five minutes later.

TTTE: *So you need me to be your fake boyfriend?*

Me: *Something like that. I know it's a lot to ask but I can pay for your train ticket and you'd get a free meal. I'm dreading turning up alone and having to face them.*

TTTE: *I would. But I'm supposed to be working at the castle on Saturday afternoon.*

Me: *Ah, right! I forgot about that. Don't worry about it then.*

TTTE: *What about Jeremy? Can't you ask him?*

Me: *No. Fuck Jeremy!!!!!*

TTTE: *What happened?!*

Me: *Let's just say I'm starting to see him more clearly and the picture isn't as pretty as I thought it was.*

There were a few minutes of nonresponse. Then I got,

TTTE: *Actually, I will come. I'll tell them I'm detained this weekend. A family emergency.*

Me: *Are you sure? That would be amazing if you could but I don't want to put you out.*

TTTE: *Yup, I'm sure. Count me in for the shit show on Saturday.*

Chapter 18

In the morning, I lent Rose one of my maid's dresses, which was slightly too tight and much too short for her but would do for the meantime. I watched as she brushed her long thick dark hair, pinning it up into a bun, ready for my second-best maid's cap. She twisted from side to side to see the effect in my looking glass, and a stab of envy penetrated my heart so painfully that I had to look away to keep from gasping.

Rose was simply stunning, but most of all, her creamy complexion was flawless. I'd never wanted anything as bad as I wanted her skin at that moment. The unfairness of it all took my breath away. We had the same colouring, eyes and hair, except that I was the ugly twin. How could God do this to me when I'd offered her charity out of the goodness of my heart? He was holding up this girl, who was so beautiful, like a reflection and was taunting me, 'See what you're never going to be?'

My life was difficult enough with Jasper at the moment, but to add Rose to the equation was simply unbearable. My mind's eye travelled into the future, and I could see with utmost certainty what was going to happen. It was inevitable: Jasper would fall in love with Rose. The fact that Rose was of the serving class didn't faze my fertile imagination. From what I knew of Jasper, he couldn't resist a pretty face, and Rose had a spunk that I was sure he'd find irresistible. I sighed in despair.

Rose turned and looked at me with concern. 'Everything all right, Mercy?' I nodded my head, already resigning myself to what lay ahead. The sooner I accepted it, the better I would be able to cope. I smiled brightly.

'Yes, let's go down and start serving breakfast.'

Maggie was putting the finishing touches on the gentlemen's breakfast of hot rolls, fresh honey, eggs, and bacon. She looked up as we entered the kitchen.

'Ahh, just in time, girls. Them's tray is ready. Mercy, do you want to carry? And, Rose, you can take in the coffee.'

I led the way, feeling as if I was about to go to the guillotine, not sure I would be able to cope with the first moment when Jasper laid eyes on Rose. But there was nothing to be done. I entered the dining room, and both he and Sebastian were there reading their papers. Only Sebastian lowered his and greeted us, though.

'Good morning, Mercy,' he said warmly. 'And this must be Rose?'

'Yes, Rose Baker, sir,' said Rose, dropping a small curtsy. 'Pleased to make your acquaintance.'

Sebastian looked at her appreciatively, taking in her pretty heart-shaped face and blooming complexion.

'Maggie tells me you're in need of employment and a place to stay for a while. Well, you're welcome here for as long as you like. I hope you don't mind sharing with Mercy?'

'No, sir, I don't mind at all,' said Rose, putting down the coffee pot on the table.

'Well, I mind,' said Jasper, lowering his paper and pouring himself a cup of coffee. 'I'm sure I don't want some half-starved, loose-fingered gypsy in the house. One loose-fingered maid is enough.'

I waited for it, any minute now. He took a bite of his roll, glanced up, and saw Rose standing there, looking more unlike a loose-fingered gypsy than anyone ever could. Chewing, his eyes widened and slid insolently from the top of her head, lingered on her rosebud lips, followed the curve of her cheek down to her slightly swelled bosom, continued down to her slim waist, and then to the tips of her dainty booted toes.

There was a silence while Jasper swallowed. I'd never seen him look so lost for words, but he quickly recovered his composure.

'Well, well, how do you do, Rose? Forgive me. I can see you're not a gypsy, anything but.' He chuckled.

Rose grinned and dropped a low curtsy. 'Pleased to meet you again, sir. We didn't get a chance to be properly introduced last night.'

Jasper looked a bit uncomfortable. 'Er, no, I was a little under the weather last night. Do forgive me.'

'Of course,' said Rose brightly. He gazed at her, a small smile playing on his lips, and I groaned inwardly.

Meanwhile, Sebastian was taking in this exchange and met my anguished eye with his sympathetic one.

Help! I implored him silently. He coughed, and the flirtatious atmosphere was instantly dispelled.

'Thank you, girls. That will be all for now,' he said. 'I've left a list of chores with Maggie. Mercy, you can get Rose acquainted with the way things are to be done.'

As we curtsied and left the room, I sensed Jasper's eyes following us, but it wasn't my back they were trained on—I was sure of that.

I was worried about Rose. The way Jasper had eyed her with barely concealed desire shot arrows of fear through my heart. Rose had made no comment or shown any sign of returning the interest, but now she knew that Jasper was soon to be rich (more fool me for telling her). Was there any reason she would resist his advances if he decided to make them?

From what I knew of Rose, she had been in trouble on at least one occasion, but perhaps there had been more. Common sense would surely prevail on her part. Why would she risk the small pocket of security she had living here? There was a very real chance that she would find herself alone, friendless, and starving in the woods again if she made any wrong move. If she became involved with Jasper, I wasn't sure I could be a stalwart friend and keep the news to myself. And I doubted Sebastian would be pleased to have his friend carrying on with one of his servants.

As the days passed and none of my fears came to pass, I relaxed. I grew used to Jasper's salivating glances whenever Rose walked into the room, and my confidence that the situation would not become more heated grew whenever she barely looked at him or answered him in curt sentences.

I knew from our conversations at night in my room that she found him 'arrogant' and 'conceited'. I didn't disagree. Jasper was all that she said. But I had found his weakness, and it had endeared him to me. It was written in a letter that I kept tucked away in an old apron at the back of my bottom dresser drawer, where no one could find it. I felt as long as I had his letter, I had some kind of control over the situation.

Then something changed. One morning, instead of answering Jasper's enquiry to her health with a curt 'Very well, sir', she blushed and lowered her eyes and barely whispered a reply.

I kept pouring Sebastian's coffee but glanced at Jasper, who smirked and bit into his toast. What was wrong with her? Was she slowly but surely falling under his spell like the rest of womankind?

In the kitchen, as we cleared away the breakfast things, she seemed subdued.

'Rose, are you all right?' I enquired tentatively. She looked at me, her expression clouded.

'I wish I were you,' she replied. I was bewildered. What girl in her right mind would ever wish to be me?

'You can't mean that,' I said stiffly.

'I do, I truly do,' she said and, without further explanation, walked out of the kitchen.

I pondered her words all morning as I went about my chores. I felt disconnected from the household, as if something were happening beyond my comprehension. I didn't see Rose again that morning to question her strange statement. In the late afternoon, I took my duster into the library room to give the books a thorough going-over as it had been a while since I had.

Part of me wasn't surprised to find Jasper there bent over Rose. She was lying awkwardly on the chaise longue, and he was kissing her neck. Her blouse was half off her shoulder, revealing an expanse of creamy white perfect flesh. The other part recoiled in horror as he murmured his appreciation and ran a hand over her bodice. I backed away slowly and carefully so as to not make a sound. The last thing I saw was Jasper hitching up her skirt to caress her white thighs and Rose, her eyes full of sorrow, looking at me over his shoulder.

I ran out of the house and into the field at the back until I reached the willow tree. My hands were shaking uncontrollably. All that I had feared was coming to pass. I breathed slowly and deeply. How Rose was acting and what she had said now made sense to me. Jasper had obviously started making advances, and she was powerless to stop him. The irony of it was that I was the one who was in love with him, and I would've changed places with her in a heartbeat.

To witness him making love to her was so painful I didn't know whether I could bear to face either of them again. Not for the first time, I felt myself to be cursed with this face that drove men away.

What earthly advantage could it possibly be to have

looks that caused pity rather than desire? Rose didn't know what she was talking about. I stayed outside under the willow until dusk fell. With a sigh, I trudged back to the house and prepared myself to face the worst: that Jasper and Rose were now in love.

In the kitchen, Maggie was preparing supper—a juicy rabbit stew by the looks of it. There was no sign of Rose. 'Mercy, there you are, love. I was wondering where you'd got to. Can you fetch Rose for me and get her to come and set the dining room table?'

With a sigh, I trudged upstairs to my bedroom. Rose was lying face down on the bed in her chemise, unmoving. She'd changed out of her maid's dress, and it was discarded on the floor in a heap.

'Rose? Maggie needs you to set the table.'

Rose didn't reply, so I went over to her and touched her on the shoulder. 'Are you asleep?' Her head moved from side to side imperceptibly.

'What's wrong then? Are you ill?' I have to say I didn't have much sympathy in me at that moment—not until she turned her face around, and I saw a giant red welt on the side of it. I gasped.

'Did Jasper do that?'

She nodded, and tears started pouring down her cheeks, following the course of those that had gone before.

'But why?' I asked, naively not believing that anything but true love could possibly come out of the encounter I had witnessed.

'Because I wouldn't give him what he wanted, that's why.' She gulped and sniffed, looking around for something to blow her nose on. I silently handed her my handkerchief.

'I saw the disappointment in your eyes, and I just couldn't let him use me like all the others had,' she said. 'So I pushed him off, and he slapped me hard to teach me a lesson.'

I sucked in my breath. I knew Jasper had a temper, but up until now, I didn't think he would physically hurt anyone.

'I don't believe it,' I said.

'Believe it,' said Rose in a harsh voice. 'Men like him want only one thing, and when they can't get it, they turn ugly. I've met his type before. Now do you know why I wish I had your pockmarks? There's no way he would've laid a finger on me if I looked like you. Sebastian probably hired you because you'd had the pox, and he knew Jasper wouldn't look at you twice. I bet he's got into trouble before.'

Her words were a sharp knife stabbing my heart. It was true—I knew it. But it still hurt.

'I would give anything to even have one murmur of

affection from his lips,' I said softly.

Rose looked at me in sudden understanding. 'You're in love with him, aren't you? Him! Oh, Mercy, no.' I didn't deny it, just looked down, ashamed.

'I can't help it,' I whispered. 'I know it's hopeless.'

'It's worse than hopeless—it's ludicrous. Him? He's a ...'

Whatever Jasper was remained unsaid as Maggie came up and banged on the door, wanting to know whether we were coming down. I made some excuse on Rose's behalf about her being ill and served supper myself to Jasper and Sebastian.

My feelings about what he had done to Rose were barely contained, though, and I couldn't help banging Jasper's plate down on the table so some of the rabbit stew splashed on his silk breeches.

'Blast! That's a clean suit, Mercy!' he exclaimed, dabbing frantically at the material with his napkin.

I shrugged.

'Well, aren't you going to apologise?' he demanded, his face reddening in outrage. I shrugged again.

Somehow, seeing the welt on Rose's face had hardened my heart, and I didn't care about his suit. I was so angry I felt like tipping the whole bowl of rabbit stew into his lap. Suit be damned.

'Sebastian, this is unacceptable behaviour from a

servant!' Jasper's voice was growing high-pitched.

'Yet striking one across the face because she resisted your advances *is* acceptable?' I interjected hotly. I was sick of staying quiet even if it meant getting myself fired.

Sebastian stared at Jasper, who had quietened down remarkably quickly. He even looked slightly remorseful.

'Jasper, is there anything you want to tell me?' Sebastian asked.

'Not with her in the room,' said Jasper grumpily, nodding in my direction.

So with that, I hastily took my leave before I did or said something I would regret further.

Chapter 19

Saturday came all too quickly for my liking, but I was relieved when I saw Thomas at the train station. He was wearing nice jeans and a black shirt; a backpack was slung over his shoulder. He broke out into a broad grin when he saw me.

'Hey,' he said and kissed me briefly on the lips like he had before. A nervous fluttery feeling descended upon my midriff. I wanted more: more kissing, more touching, more everything from him. There was definitely an attraction there, on my side anyway. For all I knew, Thomas got his kicks from helping damsels in distress deal with their dysfunctional families.

When we'd settled into our seats on the train, the inevitable question arose. 'So what went down with Jeremy to make you so anti?'

Oh, the tale I could tell! I'd debated whether to divulge any of the finer details to Thomas and had decided that I would preserve Jeremy's dignity. He was still my boss after all, and Thomas was Eleanor's cousin.

'There were certain aspects that I wasn't comfortable with as the evening progressed,' I replied. 'Please don't mention any of what I told you on the phone to Eleanor.'

'You know I won't. So the foot massage didn't go well?' he pressed, seeming super curious to know. Was he angling to find out if I'd slept with Jeremy?

'We didn't have sex if that's what you're asking.'

Was it my imagination, or did Thomas seem relieved to hear that?

'I wasn't prying,' he said smoothly. 'I just hoped it went OK for your sake. You seemed really upset about the whole whip thing. And I was a bit worried when you didn't message me after.'

I shook my head. 'Honestly, it started off OK, but it went downhill rapidly when I found out some ... things about him. And now he's going to hire Irish Lucy as my research assistant.'

Thomas raised an eyebrow. 'Irish Lucy?'

'Blonde, big tits—my worst nightmare. He was interviewing her in his office the other day and pretty much ignored me completely.'

Thomas took my hand and squeezed it. 'I'm sorry.'

'Now I can't even enjoy a nice evening with my fake boyfriend because my awful sister and cheating ex will be there.'

He chuckled and kept hold of my hand. I assumed he was getting into his fake boyfriend role, but his large warm hand around mine felt lovely anyway.

'Thanks for this and for taking time off work. I owe you big time.'

He shrugged. 'Been thinking I might cut down on the guide work anyway. It'd be nice to have one day free on the weekend.'

'What would you do with your day off?'

'Dunno. Go for a bike ride maybe.' He paused. 'If I did, would you come too?'

I shifted in my seat. Well, we were sort of friends now. Hanging out with Thomas on the odd occasion wouldn't be the worst thing in the world. It was nice to know he was thinking longer term. 'Perhaps. If it wasn't raining.'

* * *

It was an eight-minute stroll from Paddington Station to Cleveland Square, where my mother's flat was situated. I could tell Thomas was impressed by the way he was looking around at the white-stucco-fronted mansions with their porticos.

It was a nice area all right, and at any other time, I would've been enjoying the visit. But knowing that in a few minutes' time I would be facing my sister and ex was causing me to freak out. What with the Jeremy date being a flop and reading about Mercy's issues with Jasper and Rose, everything was getting a bit much.

I scrabbled in the pocket of my overnight bag for the key I'd stashed in there in case I needed a breather.

'Thomas, do you mind if we sit in the park for a bit before we go in?'

He stopped and glanced at the leafy park we were walking adjacent to. 'Sure, but it looks private.'

'It is, residents only. But my mother gave me a copy of her key.' I held it up to show him.

Thomas looked doubly impressed. 'Nice!'

Inside the garden, I made a beeline for the nearest park bench. There wasn't anyone around apart from a couple of girls chatting on a blanket in the late-afternoon sunshine. I sat down and stuck my head between my legs.

'Whoa, are you OK?' asked Thomas worriedly.

'No, I'm not looking forward to this.'

He sat down beside me and placed a hand on the middle of my back, resting it there.

'Just breathe for a bit, in and out. That's it.' Tears pricked my eyes at his kindness. 'You know we could always blow the whole thing off and book into a hotel. Grab dinner, watch a movie, and chill,' he added.

The thought of that was hugely tempting. I took one last deep breath and sat up. 'I can't. I have to face them.' A tear overflowed and ran down my cheek before I could wipe it away.

'Come here.'

Thomas gathered me into his arms, and I laid my head on his shoulder as he rubbed my back. I couldn't help crying a little. It had been so long since anyone had held me like this.

'You know you're pretty brave, don't you?' he murmured.

I sniffed. 'So brave that I coerced you into coming with me.'

'You didn't coerce me. I wanted to.'

It wasn't an admission of his feelings, but I could hear it in the tender tone of his voice and by the way he was holding me, like I was a fragile flower he was scared of crushing. I'm not sure how it had happened or what I'd done, but Thomas *cared* about me, and I felt like I might care about him too. It seemed to put things into perspective.

I lifted my head to look at him. He smiled, then kissed me gently on my temple, my cheek, then my lips; and I knew that what we were feeling for each other wasn't fake at all— it was very real. We kissed as the breeze ruffled the leaves on the trees, and I felt the warmth of the sun and the heat of his body melding into mine; it was a deep, sweet kiss, and I didn't want it to end.

But then Thomas hugged me tightly and said, 'I'd much rather sit here and kiss you. But if you're feeling better, we should probably face the villainous couple or, as I'm now thinking of them, Evil 1 and Evil 2.'

I laughed at that, liking that he'd said 'we'. 'I think maybe now I can.'

***

My mother was an avid collector of Art Deco furniture. Her flat was *busy*, but nothing like Jeremy's haphazard jumble. There was room to move around at least. But I noticed a side table in the entryway that hadn't been there last time I visited.

'Is that new?' I asked, kissing her cheek as she waved me into the flat.

'Yes, it's French. Karelian birch,' she said, and was about to shut the door but saw Thomas waiting behind me, carrying his backpack in his hand. Her eyes widened, realising that he wasn't someone delivering takeaway pamphlets, that he was with me.

'Oh, I'm sorry! Do come in.'

'Mum, this is my boyfriend, Thomas ...' I began, then

realised I didn't actually know his last name.

'Coggeshall,' he supplied, pronouncing it 'cog-shawl'. 'It's Old English, from a town in Essex,' he added as if we might be wondering.

I looked at him in surprise. 'Coggeshall is near Braintree, where Mercy lived at the rectory. How strange!'

'Who's Mercy?' asked my mother, looking between us curiously.

'It's a long story.'

'Well, nice to meet you, Thomas Coggeshall. I didn't know Anna had a boyfriend, but you're very welcome.'

She gave me a piercing look, and I shifted uncomfortably. Hopefully, she wouldn't ask too many awkward questions about Thomas because I was only just getting to know him myself.

'You can leave your bags there by the stairs. Come through to the lounge. We're having an aperitif before dinner.' She floated off in a cloud of Chanel.

Thomas looked at me. 'All good?'

I nodded. 'Though I feel like I should reapply my mascara after the freak-out. Do I look like a panda?' Luckily, his shirt was black; otherwise, he'd have black smears on his shoulder.

He leaned forward to inspect my eyes, wiped at the edge of one with his thumb, then gave me a swift kiss on the cheek. 'You look great. Should we walk in together holding hands?'

'Yes, if that's OK?'

'Fine by me.' He caught my sweaty hand in his less-sweaty one, and we approached the lounge, looking for all the world like we were an established couple. Having him support me in my time of need was a big deal and so nice of him. I didn't think I could've faced my sister and ex alone, unless I was extremely drunk.

Here we go, I thought as we went through into the light, bright lounge that looked out onto the greenery of Cleveland Square. My stomach dipped as I braced myself to see the man who'd cheated on me and barely offered an explanation for his actions. But the lounge was empty apart from my mother, sitting in a cream round-armed chair. The matching cream buttoned sofa had no one on it.

I looked around the room as if they might have been hiding behind one of the potted palms, about to jump out. But there was no sign of them.

'Is it only us?'

'Beth is in the kitchen fixing some G and Ts.'

My heart sank. So she was here.

'Just to warn you, you'll need to tread carefully,' my mother said in a confidential tone.

'How come?'

'Are you talking about me? I'm right here, you know,' said a voice from behind my left shoulder. I slowly turned to see my sister, Beth, standing in the doorway. She was clutching an antique gilt tray with several glasses and a tall blue bottle of Bombay Sapphire.

Seeing her again after everything that had happened was shocking. She stalked into the lounge and tossed her long dark hair as she went past, almost smacking me in the face with it. I smelt her familiar lilac perfume—it smelt like betrayal.

'You might as well sit down instead of standing there, gawking,' she said, placing the tray on the oval coffee table and taking the other round-armed chair.

Thomas and I promptly sat on the couch opposite.

He looked at her and looked at me, his mouth slightly ajar. Beth was my spitting image; we were identical twins after all. We even dressed similarly. Today I was wearing black tailored pants and a cream silk top. She had on black tailored pants and a mauve silk top. Beth's favourite colour was purple because she liked to think of herself as a spiritual person. Our long dark hair was long and loose, though she had a feathery side fringe. Her face and nose were slightly narrower.

She waved a hand at the tray of drinks. 'Help yourselves. I brought out the bottle if you need it stronger. God knows I do.' She collected a glass of G and T from the tray and sat back in the chair, crossing her legs. Then she eyed Thomas with interest. 'Who're you?'

Oh no, no way. She was not going to have him too! Wasn't one boyfriend enough? And where the hell was Ben?

'I'm Thomas, Anna's boyfriend. And you are?' he said politely, and I could've kissed him right there and then.

'Beth,' she said, sounding a bit rattled.

'Where's Ben?' I asked. 'Upstairs?'

My mother shook her head slightly at me as Beth sipped her drink, her forehead scrunching until her dark salon-shaped eyebrows almost met in the middle.

'He's only gone and dumped me,' she spat.

I blew out my cheeks and grabbed the gin bottle. I was definitely going to need my G and T stronger.

***

'Why didn't you tell me they'd broken up?' I whispered to my mother in the kitchen after we'd had our beef bourguignon. I'd reluctantly left Thomas with Beth in the dining room so I could help clear the dishes. I fervently hoped he'd still be there (and still mine) when I went back in.

'Today was the first I'd heard of it. She turned up here

alone and said he'd left her. It must've happened quite recently. Poor thing,' my mother replied. 'Thomas is nice, though. Where did you meet him?'

'Er, on an Oxford Castle tour.'

Apparently, Beth had been asking Thomas the same thing as they were discussing it when I came back in with a plate of profiteroles.

Beth looked up at me with gin-soaked eyes and giggled. 'Maybe I need to come to Oxford and go on this tour so I can meet a nice guy too,' she slurred.

'I think you've had enough,' I said, removing the Bombay Sapphire out of her reach.

'Aw, come on, Anna. Lighten up. Thomas has probably got a brother or a cousin I can hang out with.'

'No,' I said firmly. 'He doesn't.'

'For God's sake, don't tell me you're still angry about Ben? That was years ago.' She pouted, biting delicately into a profiterole. 'He's dumped me too. That makes us even. So you can stop playing the moral high ground and bloody well forgive me.'

I was too stunned to say anything.

But Thomas wasn't so speech-impaired. 'Beth, I don't know the exact details of what took place when Ben broke up with Anna and decided to go off with you. That's because she's polite and nice and doesn't tell tales,' he said evenly. 'But I know what you did hurt her deeply, so deeply that she was dreading coming here tonight and seeing you. And now I know why.'

Beth didn't say anything. She licked cream off her finger sullenly.

'And for the record, I don't think she should forgive you. But I hope she forgives herself because she deserves so much better from someone who's her own flesh and blood.'

Thomas got up from the table and went into the kitchen, where I heard him running the tap to get a glass of water.

I blinked my eyes as they'd started brimming again. Thomas was really setting me off lately. And oh god, what he'd said was amazing. Hastily, I grabbed a couple of profiteroles, feeling like I'd rather spend the evening with him than listen to my sister's drunken bleating.

'I think it's best if we eat these in our room. Thanks for dinner, Mum,' I said and exited too, leaving a stony silence behind me.

He was right: some things in life were unforgivable.

Chapter 20

The red mark on Rose's face had calmed down by later that evening, but I hadn't. My emotions were whirring around in me too fast and violent to be tamed. I sat on the bed. I paced. I sat. I paced. Rose didn't know what to do with me.

'I don't think he'll come after me again if that's what you're worried about,' she said, twisting a length of hair around her finger. 'After what you said in the dining room, I'm sure Sebastian has told him to stay away from me.'

'It's not you I'm worried about—it's me,' I said worriedly. 'You didn't see his face. He hates me even more than he did before, if that's possible.'

'Oh, Mercy,' Rose sighed, getting into bed. 'I'm sure he doesn't hate you. He's just annoyed that he got caught out. Why don't you come to bed and get some rest? It's been an eventful day.'

I got into bed, but I couldn't sleep. I was wound up like a tightly coiled spring. Images of Jasper and Rose went round and round in my head until I couldn't stand it anymore. When I heard that Rose was asleep, I got out of bed and left the room.

Of all the reckless notions I'd had recently, this was perhaps the craziest and most dangerous. But such was the madness of love. I couldn't seem to control my actions. I needed to go to him. Like I had in my dream, I slipped down the dark narrow stairwell and along the hallway. I turned Jasper's door handle and stepped into his room. The moonlight showed a shape underneath the covers, breathing steadily. I went over and knelt next to the bed so the light was behind me, but full upon Jasper's perfect sleeping face. Forgetting the ugly scene at supper and all his slights towards me, in that moment, all I could see was beauty, and my heart expanded with love.

As if feeling my presence, Jasper stirred and woke. 'Rose?' he murmured sleepily. 'Is that you?'

I didn't correct him, although I knew it was wrong of me. As in my dream, his hand grasped my wrist and he pulled me into bed with him, down into the soft covers and his warm embrace. I was so startled with joy I could hardly think. I felt like I was in heaven. He nuzzled my neck and whispered sweet nothings, and I was so happy I didn't even stop to think they were meant for another.

'Oh, Jasper,' I whispered, and he began to kiss me. But as he did so, he brushed one hand along my cheekbone. Midstroke, after feeling the pockmarks on my face, his hand froze. Jasper recoiled with a gasp of horror when he realised it was me he was kissing and not his beloved Rose. He inched away from me as far as he could up against the headboard and scrubbed at his mouth with the back of his hand. This made me angry.

'I'm not infectious, Jasper. Don't you know anything about the pox? Once you've had it, you can never have it again.' I crawled over to him in the hope he would resume his affection, but he sprung out of bed.

'How dare you come in here and pretend to be Rose! Do you really think I would've kissed you if I'd known it was you?' he said icily, snatching up a blanket from the chair.

Before I knew what was happening, he'd thrown the blanket over my head and wrestled me off the bed to the ground. There was a moment of disbelief before fear kicked in, and then I struggled with all my might, feeling that he would smother me to death. I screamed for Sebastian and managed to free a foot and strike Jasper in the shin. He grunted, let go of an edge, and I scrambled out. Grabbing his whip lying on the dresser, I brought it down with all my might on his back. But he grabbed my ankle, trying to pull my leg out from under me. I screamed again, full force, and sharply kicked him in the nether regions. He collapsed with a yell of pain.

I heard running feet along the corridor, and Sebastian burst into the room in his nightshirt.

'What on earth's going on in here?' he exclaimed, staring

at Jasper lying on the floor, holding his crotch and groaning. I threw myself into Sebastian's arms.

'H-he tried to kill me!' I whimpered.

'Is this true, Jasper?' asked Sebastian, sounding incredulous.

'She came in here without invitation, Seb, and climbed into bed with me! What, pray tell, was I meant to do? I was only defending myself from the pox!'

Sebastian made a strangled noise and drew me hurriedly from the room. I couldn't stop crying and shaking from the shock of Jasper hating me that much he would try to kill me. Sebastian took me to his own room and bade me to sit on his bed.

'Oh, child,' he sighed. 'You shouldn't have done that. Jasper is deathly afraid of the pox, as you've just discovered. I've told him to get inoculated, but he's too afraid of being in any contact with the disease for that. Still, that's no excuse for what he did to you.'

He sat and put his arm around me, but still, I shook. Was it fear that had made Jasper try to snuff the life out of me or a darker part of his nature? I didn't want to wait around and find out. I no longer felt safe in this house. Whatever feelings of belonging I'd had in the rectory were gone; the spell was broken. I got up off the bed and stood looking down at Sebastian. He might be the kindest man I'd known apart from my father, but he was Jasper's friend and would always forgive him for whatever wrongs he did to me.

'Thank you, sir. I will go to my room now. I am sorry for disturbing your sleep.'

'Get some rest, Mercy, and we'll say no more about it. I'm sure Jasper will calm down and forget about it shortly.' He smiled and patted my hand.

On the way back to my room, I tried to believe Sebastian was right, but I couldn't. There was no way on earth Jasper would ever forget this, so how could I remain here?

But somehow, by confronting him, I had given myself the gift of choice. I now found myself standing at a crossroads. One path loomed before me strange, mysterious, and unthinkable in its daring. The other led to whatever pain Jasper chose to throw my way when he recovered.

Breathing heavily with a mixture of emotion and excitement, I ran up the stairs to my room and upon entering, lit a candle. Rose didn't stir. I grabbed her stolen clothing from the dresser; a shirt, a fine embroidered waistcoat and a pair of breeches that had all been freshly washed, and had scrubbed up rather well now they weren't caked in dirt. I put them on, along with my stockings and sturdy boots. Then her hat, tucking up my long dark hair so it was out of sight. I caught a glimpse of myself in the looking glass. In the flickering gloom, I looked like a young gentleman—my pox scars lending an authenticity to the illusion that Rose's perfect complexion never could.

I laughed softly to myself.

Rose woke up then and stared at me, her eyes widening when she saw me wearing her costume.

'Wha ... ?' she started. I hastily went to her bedside.

'I'm leaving, Rose,' I whispered. 'Hush now. It's for the best,' I added as she started to protest.

'But where will you go? What will you do?' A plan came fully formed to my mind, as if it had been there all along waiting for me to see it.

'I'm going to a place where my face will not cause hate as it does here.'

Rose started to cry. 'But you will be hurt. It is dangerous out there!' I smiled wryly at this.

'I believe it is more dangerous at this moment for me to stay at the rectory. Don't worry, I'll cut my hair short and the pox will keep any men's hand's from me as you said yourself. Now dry your tears and please tell Sebastian that I ... No, wait. I will write him a note before I go and leave it on his desk. Take care, Rose. You will be safe with Sebastian watching out for you.'

Rose wiped her eyes on the sheet and hopped out of bed. 'If you must go, take this at least!'

She thrust her butcher's knife into my hand, and I stowed

it in my rucksack (thinking it would be useful for hacking off my hair), along with my leather money purse and a few other belongings. I blew her a kiss and left her looking after me like a startled rabbit, but it had to be done. I felt no fear, only a strange kind of determination. I slunk quietly down the stairs and padded along the dark hallway and down the main staircase. Sebastian's study lay in pitch-blackness, but dawn was near as I could hear a few birds tweeting outside in the stillness. I lit a candle and hurriedly scratched a note with his quill. My writing was not as good as my reading, but I hoped he'd be able to understand it.

Dear Sir (Sebastian),

I am leaving to the one place where I won't cause you any more trouble. You have helped me find it by teaching me to read and I thank you from the bottom of my heart. Please give Jasper his letter, I took it without meaning to hurt him but he needs it back. Do not fret about me, I have enough money for my passage and will be safe with God looking out for me, like He has always done. Tell Maggie goodbye and I will write to mother soon and inform her of my change in circumstance. Watch over Rose!

Your maid and friend,
Mercy Graham

Tears welled in my eyes, but I held them back and carefully placed Jasper's letter on top of my own, laying beside them the slim green novel that had taught me everything I needed to know about travelling to Venice. My goodbye written, I strode purposefully to the kitchen before I changed my mind. I took down my cloak for the last time but left my basket where it was on the floor. The sound of Maggie's soft snores floated out from her room, and I could smell the faint stale odour of the previous night's rabbit stew. The breakfast things lay carefully prepared on the counter. I hovered, savouring the familiar space soon to become a mere memory.

As I turned the handle of the back door and stepped out into the cold air, how right and good it felt to leave—to make my own destiny, come what may. I thought my father too would want me to be happy and not blame myself any longer for causing his death.

I could sense his presence as I swerved off the servants' path onto the gravel drive. My boots made a satisfying crunching noise as I walked towards the road and freedom. From now on, I would create my own path. A strong feeling passed through me that everything would be all right despite the uncertainty I now faced. I had money, a destination, and my pox-scarred face was my protection.

At the end of the drive, I turned and looked back at the rectory. Rosy streaks were appearing on the horizon, but Jasper's room lay in darkness. As I watched, I thought, but could not be sure, that his curtain twitched slightly.

I turned again, thrust my icy hands deep into my coat pockets, and started walking into town to hitch a ride on a cart to Dover—my heart beating in anticipation of the journey ahead. My warm breath left white puffs of frosty air hanging in the wake of my passing. Then just like me, they were gone.

Chapter 21

'You didn't have to say anything,' I said to Thomas when we'd dumped our bags in the guest room. 'Beth was only being mouthy because she was drunk.'

He sat on the double bed, nibbling on the profiterole I'd given him. 'Yes, I did. She was pissing me off. I can't believe your sister looks so much like you, but she's so awful. How come you got all the nice genes?'

I shrugged. 'Maybe she has Dad's personality. He left when we were little, so we don't know much about him. Mum always told us he'd run away to join the circus. But when we were older, she admitted he'd skipped off to Birmingham with another woman.'

'Lordy, families,' Thomas said with a sigh.

'Oh well, at least we got through dinner. And ... and I did like what you said—about not forgiving her, but forgiving myself for not deserving better.'

I walked over to where he was sitting. 'I've realised that letting go of Jeremy is part of that because he's never going to be able to give me the kind of love that I want—a love that's reciprocated. And due to that, I've started looking for another job.'

Thomas let out a breath. 'Bravo, Anna.'

'But letting go of Jeremy is hard for me,' I said, trying not to let my voice wobble. 'I've been loving him for so long that not having him to love feels like losing my right arm. Does that make sense?'

Thomas bobbed his head. 'Sure. But you have a lot of love to give, and he doesn't deserve you.'

I laughed a little. 'No one seems to deserve me in your eyes.'

Thomas drew me down onto his lap, and I put my arms around him. 'Well, maybe ... me?' he said tentatively.

'I thought you weren't able to help me with the love part, only the sex part.'

He kissed my forehead. 'Hmm, I think I might have to extend my services where you're concerned. You can officially love me all you want.'

'Oh boy,' I said, shaking my head. 'You have no idea what you're in for. Get ready for crazy Anna love.'

Thomas grinned and caressed my cheek with his thumb. 'Lay it on me, baby. I can handle the crazy.'

* * *

I wrapped the small dark-green novel with the gilt-tooled floral border carefully in acid-free tissue paper and placed it spine down in the box along with the other books. Then I added foam cushioning, packing it in tightly so they wouldn't move around during transit. Lastly, I secured the flaps with several layers of packing tape.

Picking up the box, I manoeuvred around Becca's empty chair, pushing it closer to the desk, which had been cleared of her personal effects. She'd left last week, so I'd had the office to myself—a reprieve before Irish Lucy started, as I knew she must.

Holding the box close to my chest, I navigated the hallway, glad that Jeremy's office wasn't too far away as the damn thing was heavy. Resting the box on my knee for a few seconds, I rapped on his door.

'Come in, Anna,' intoned Jeremy's deep voice from within. But this time, I didn't feel the usual shiver down my spine. I felt, well, nothing really.

'Here are the books,' I said without waiting for him to notice me. 'They're all packed up and ready to go.' I set them down by the door in the same place I'd picked them up all those weeks ago, before I'd even met Thomas. Just thinking about him made me smile.

'You know you can still change your mind,' said Jeremy. 'I haven't started interviewing yet.'

I straightened up and looked at him. For once, he wasn't tapping or reading on his laptop; he was frowning, looking genuinely worried that he was losing his number one researcher, which he was.

'How am I going to finish my book now? I need your help.'

'No you don't,' I said. 'I've made meticulous notes. Everything is there in the Google Drive folder named POX. Plus you've got Lucy now. She's worked on several publications before, and she knows her stuff. Just promote her as soon as she starts and hire one of the other candidates as her assistant if she needs one.'

Jeremy tapped his finger on the desk, and I could see his mind whirring—if he promoted Lucy to senior researcher, it meant cosy working lunches in his office.

'You know, that might work out well,' he said, his forehead smoothing.

I smiled benignly. 'I thought it might.'

'I hope you're not leaving because of what happened ... with us,' he said suddenly. 'I never should've invited you out for dinner. Or back to my house. Or let you massage my feet. God.' He cringed.

'Well, you didn't force me. I did offer to massage them,' I teased. 'No, it's for the best. It's time I moved on. Besides, I'm looking forward to the challenges of my new job.'

And it's more money, and I'll be spending most of my time in the Radcliffe Camera ...

I turned to grasp the door handle to leave, and Jeremy said, 'I'm sorry, Anna.'

I stiffened momentarily and blinked. 'For what?'

'For not being the relationship type. I *am* fond of you,' he said gently.

A jolt of awareness went through me at his words—it appeared Jeremy had known that I was in love with him all along. His ego had maybe even enjoyed the attention. In the end, I hadn't been able to keep it a secret. After all, I did tend to wear my heart on my sleeve, as Thomas said. Before, I probably would've turned beetroot red and wished the floor would swallow me whole, but things were different now. I wondered if I should tell him that 'fond' really wasn't good enough for me. But what was the point? So I ignored it and reiterated, 'You'll be fine with Lucy. She's good at her job.'

And whatever happens with you and her, I'm glad I won't be there to witness it.

'Just, for God's sake, promise me you'll call that cleaning company. I sent you their details.'

Jeremy laughed and gave me a small salute. 'Promise!'

I took one last look at his office and at him: wood, paper, glass, warmth, and beauty.

Chapter 22

After I left the rectory, I made my way to the place that I believed would not scorn me—the most serene city of masks. However, my journey from Braintree to Dover by horse and cart, and then onto Venice by various ships and stagecoaches was long, tedious and not without incident.

I had been right that travelling as a young gentleman would afford me protection. If anyone enquired as to my business, I simply lowered my voice and said gruffly that I was on a grand tour of Europe and moved on. However, despite this, and as well as cutting off my hair, on the passage from Marseille to Genoa, my true identity was revealed by an overly friendly young woman who had who taken a liking to me and peered too closely at my chest.

Outraged that I was posing as a gentleman and had "tricked" her, she hauled me to the captain and demanded I be arrested. Yet, he took pity on me after I pleaded with him and he said I could be his maid instead. But it was more of a punishment as I had wear an ugly dress and do various chores on the ship, including serving him food and washing his disgusting feet!

After a miserable couple of days of this, I was up on deck, scrubbing it or some such; and a bored upper-class lady sat nearby to look out at the ocean. She must have heard my sighs and, since she was looking for amusement, bade me to tell her my story. Which I did, leaving out no parts of it, including having the pox, being hired as a maid, Sebastian teaching me to read and write, falling in love with Jasper, him trying to kill me, finding Rose in the woods, dressing as a man, and now being the captain's maid.

Lady Villiers-Cadogan, as she told me her name was, looked astonished at hearing all this and seemed highly entertained. Being mindful of my present unwholesome circumstances, she said I could travel with her to Venice in her private carriage when we docked and that she would be able to help me with a position. Apparently, she was betrothed to a nobleman, Conte Mocenigo, and would be in need of an English maid, being unable to speak Italian herself. There was another role she had in mind for me as well.

She said that Conte Mocenigo's first wife had died of the pox a few years ago and that he had a son, Francesco, who was now 21. He had contracted the pox at the same time as his mother and been left with severe pockmarks but was otherwise unharmed. The count required someone as a companion for his son as he did not go out much into society, and he feared he was becoming lonely. Francesco, apparently, was also quite learned and had taught himself a little English and wanted to improve his skills.

Lady Villiers-Cadogan said that I would be perfect for this task and that Francesco would benefit because I not only was near his own age but also shared his affliction.

When we arrived in Venice, I was grateful to the lady for giving me a position; and when I first met Francesco, I thought he was handsome despite his scars. He was similarly taken with me (something I found out afterwards).

After spending time with him for many hours and helping him to read and speak English, we became firm friends. Every day, we enjoyed conversing, strolling in the shady parts of the garden, and generally being in each other's company. One day, he held my hand and kissed it. On another occasion, he picked me a flower and tucked it behind my ear. Slowly but surely, because our hearts were true beneath our pockmarked skin, we fell in love.

When Francesco proposed, going down on one knee in the garden, where the scarlet roses bloomed, it was the happiest moment of my life. We were given his father's blessing to marry since he saw how joyful his son was and as he himself was happy with the match he had made with Lady Villiers-Cadogan. I knew my situation was special and somewhat strange, for it would be unheard-of in England for such a thing to occur between a maid and a nobleman.

But in Venice, it seemed some rules were made to be broken.

Our wedding was during Carnevale; and after we were joined at the church, there was a celebration back at the palazzo, where everyone dined and danced wearing exquisite costumes and masks. It was divine, and I felt like I was where I truly belonged, with the people of La Serenissima.

After being married for some months, I conceived and gave birth to a girl and then again to a boy. Our two children, Arianna (named after Francesco's mother) and Giovanni (named after my father), are asleep in the room next door. When they were of age, at my insistence, both were inoculated. For I did not want them to suffer, like Francesco and I had suffered, with the pox.

My dear one is sleeping as I write this at the desk. It is still early, and I'm looking out our bedroom window as the sun rises and the lapping waters of the Grand Canal turn pink, blue, and gold. Sometimes I catch sight of my reflection in the water or a looking glass, but I can now look upon myself without flinching, for my husband tells me every day that I am beautiful. I have finally come to accept that I am worthy of his love, even as a pox-scarred contessa. That is another thing that took me a while to get used to as it is quite the step up in status! But my new title has given me the means to provide for my mother and sister back in England better than I ever could as a maid; they shall not want for anything as long as they live.

Sebastian and I still correspond on occasion, and he mentioned in his last letter that Maggie is well and that Rose had had a third child (she ended up marrying the gardner's son, and now her husband comes weekly to rake the drive and clip the box hedge) and that Jasper and Arabella had married. I thought I would feel pain at this news, but to my surprise, I didn't. I wish Jasper well, for having Arabella as a wife is punishment enough for anyone. And I know, in some way, the pox was the cause of making us both crazed: I with needing his love and he with grief for his family. But it does make me smile that he considered me so lowly, and here I am now, a contessa! If I had only known then what fate had in store for me, I would have felt more at ease with my circumstances at the rectory!

Nevertheless, when this book is published, I shall send Sebastian a copy for his library room. It pleases me to think of it sitting in there alongside Lord Alby's and of Sebastian taking it out to read from time to time, chuckling to himself and thinking fondly of our time together.

I have written this account of what took place at the rectory with Jasper not as a cautionary tale (for I did not have a choice in living in the same house as him), but to serve as a comfort for those that may find themselves in the same impossible situation of unrequited love.

You are not alone, and God will find a way to help you even if all seems hopeless. And when He gives you that opportunity, you must seize it with both hands and run to your freedom without looking back, for true love awaits at your journey's end.

Peace be with you,
Contessa Mercy Mocenigo,
Venice, 1776

Chapter 23

I thought I would be more upset about leaving Jeremy, but the only feeling I had was relief. I was free of him. I had left my broken and bruised heart in the pages of that small green book, and I didn't want it anymore. Jeremy could go on dating every woman in Oxford, and I wouldn't be there to see it. Besides, tonight, I had an after-work date of my own. I was meeting my boyfriend at Queen's Lane Coffee House.

There was a certain irony that Thomas wanted to meet here. Not only was it where Eleanor first introduced me to the idea of dating her 'attractive' cousin. It was also fitting because I'd just started working on a two-year research project on the Tudor queens under Professor Jane Smalley. When the respected academic with a string of letters after her name had chosen me and a couple of others out of a long list of applicants, it had been a sweet karmic moment. Apparently, it was my paper on Queen Mary II that had clinched it; she'd been impressed and described it as 'outstanding'.

Thomas was at the counter, gazing up at the menu, when I snaked an arm around his waist.

'I hope that's Anna Butler because if it's not, then it could be awkward,' he said.

'It's me,' I replied, tilting my head to receive his kiss.

'What would you like? Latte? Cappuccino?'

'Hmm, I've decided to give up coffee for a bit. I might have peppermint tea.'

When Thomas had ordered and we were sipping our drinks at a table in the corner, he asked, 'So you never told me how it went with Jeremy. Did he cry and beg you not to leave?'

'No crying, but there was a little bit of begging.'

Thomas gave the briefest of smiles. 'How do you feel about leaving? Bereft?'

Thomas was a confident guy, but even I could tell he was subtly checking that I was over Jeremy. He didn't have to worry.

'Strangely enough, not really. I was sadder finishing Mercy's memoir and packing it away, knowing that it was going to sit on a shelf in a library archive and no one else might read it for decades.'

'Yeah, that is slightly depressing.'

'At least she'll get a mention in Jeremy's book. I gave him a ton of notes highlighting how the pox had affected her life, physically and emotionally. So hopefully, they make it into the final version, though I didn't put too much detail about Jasper.'

'What happened with her and him in the end?' asked

Thomas curiously.

'Well, after nearly raping Rose, he tried to kill Mercy. But she managed to get away from him.'

Thomas shook his head. 'Jesus, that dude. He needed to be locked up.'

'It all turned out OK. She moved to Venice, married a rich count, and had two children. And she wrote a book to comfort people suffering from unrequited love. It helped me at the time to know that someone else had been through it too. I'm glad I'm cured, though. That *you* cured me.'

'You're welcome. It was a tough assignment, but one I gladly undertook, especially since it helped you get over your sex phobia.' Thomas's mouth quirked. 'But I'm glad to hear that Mercy found happiness and fulfilment in the end.' He tipped his cup to finish the dregs of his latte. 'Hey, do you want to come to my place for dinner? You'll have to excuse the mess in the kitchen, though. I haven't tidied for a few days.'

I hid a smile, thinking that however messy Thomas thought his kitchen was, it would never in a million years rival Jeremy's pigsty.

'Definitely,' I said happily. 'And I can tell you all about my new project.'

'Yeah, I've been wanting to hear about that. Sounds awesome,' he said, nuzzling his cheek against mine.

Of the many and varied things I loved about Thomas Coggeshall, the one I loved most was that he enjoyed discussing history. He didn't even mind if it spilled over to pillow talk. That night, after making sweet, passionate love, we had a long and in-depth discussion about Anne Boleyn. But I knew he indulged me in my latest obsession with the Tudor queens because he loved me, and knowing that he reciprocated my feelings was a daily joy. Just like Mercy over two centuries ago, I had seized freedom with both hands and discovered that true love did indeed await at my journey's end.

~ THE END ~

Afterword

Smallpox was one of the deadliest infectious diseases in human history. It had no cure. Inoculation, while providing immunity from variola major, was dangerous if not administered properly; and deaths did still occur (one in fifty, as opposed to three in ten from catching it naturally).

However, in 1796, an English doctor, Edward Jenner, made a radical discovery. Milkmaids who'd had cowpox were immune to the smallpox virus. He experimented by scraping small amounts of the cowpox virus into tiny incisions on a patient's arm. Although producing a fever and slight unwellness, the patient recovered with no ill effects and was thereafter immune to smallpox.

Jenner's insistence that cowpox was less infectious than smallpox and could be administered to prevent the full-blown disease was proved to be correct time and time again when all his subjects successfully resisted smallpox. This groundbreaking work led to the development of an official smallpox vaccine, which saved the lives of millions and laid the foundation for modern immunisation practices.

The dreaded 'Speckled Monster' of Mercy's day no longer exists in modern society. Thanks to the tireless persistence of the World Health Organization, smallpox was declared eradicated in 1980. Only two highly secure medical research centres have stockpiles of the virus: one in Koltsovo in Russia and one in Atlanta in the United States.

Also by Angela

Brontë Lovers

The Holly Project

You Had Me at Ice Cream

I'll Meet You in Florence

The House of Dating Disasters

My Double Life

Travel & Mayhem

3 Book Rom-Com Collection

All books available on Amazon and Kindle Unlimited

Acknowledgements

Thank you for reading *POX*. I hope you enjoyed it! If so, I'd be thrilled if you left a review or star rating on Amazon and/or Goodreads. Your feedback truly makes a difference and helps this indie author's journey immensely.

I'm grateful for having a team of people to help me on the publishing journey. Thank you to my beta readers, Katy Hristova, Katharen Martin, Sarah Williamson, and Joanna Woollcombe-Gosson, for your insights and encouraging comments on the first draft. Thanks to my copyeditor Peachy Yap and to My Lan Khuc Valle for your amazing cover art. Lastly, thanks to my partner Chris Lambert, your sense of humour is infectious!

If you listen to Spotify, check out the POX playlist at

➜ angelapearse.pub/book-spotify-playlists

To receive alerts on upcoming releases,
sign up to my newsletter at

➜ angelapearse.pub

About the Author

ANGELA PEARSE writes quirky romantic comedies that capture the humour of everyday life. A freelance editor with an MA in English, she enjoys travelling, hiking, cooking, binge-watching Netflix, and reading copious amounts of chick lit. Originally from New Zealand, Angela currently lives in Edinburgh with her partner. Visit angelapearse.pub.